SHADOW HOUR

SHADOW CELL BOOK 3

ERNEST DEMPSEY

138 PUBLISHING

This one's for all the girls out there. Be strong. Be smart. Be brave. Be resilient. Be awesome. Be anything you want to be.

JOIN THE ADVENTURE

Join the Ernest Dempsey VIP reader list to get exclusive free content, updates on new releases, and to interact with the author. Click here to join for FREE: ernestdempsey.net.

1

LIVERPOOL, PRESENT DAY

One second the building was there. The next, it was gone, consumed by white-hot fire. Searing sparks scorched the air, leaving threadlike trails of smoke in their wake.

There was no screaming, no survivors emerging from the smoldering rubble. Anyone who'd been inside was dead, their life snuffed out in a violent explosion, erased as if they were nothing more than a graphite sketch on paper.

The JW-670 bomb was designed to pierce a building's outer shell, up to a thickness of four feet, and delivering a secondary inner warhead that would burrow another foot into the next layer—usually a ground floor—before detonating. Such a weapon ensured that not only the structure above the surface would be destroyed but that most basement facilities would be heavily damaged as well. The JW-670 could penetrate almost any ordinary structure and most military installations with severe efficiency.

"That certainly did the job." A man in the corner spoke with an English accent. He wore the uniform of a high-ranking British military commander. Medals dangled from his chest pockets as he spoke.

"Indeed, sir." June Holiday gave a curt nod.

June didn't like being around top brass. They were demanding and irrational, a combination that caused more problems than it solved. She'd been the point person on more Shadow Cell missions than anyone else in the ultra-covert agency and commanded respect all the way to the top. That included the prime minister of Great Britain and the president of the United States.

Having to rely on military personnel meant bringing in a man like the general standing across from her. His bald, splotchy head gleamed under the recessed lighting. There were a few strands of hair clinging on for dear life around his ears and at the back of his skull. She'd often wondered what the point was of holding on to those last scraps of hair. She supposed it added a hint of maturity or dignity. It wasn't important, so she let the thought go. Right now, only one thing was important: the target had been eliminated.

"That should be the last of them—if your source is correct." The general twisted his head and looked over his shoulder to where an old man sat in the shadows. His face was consumed by the darkness; only his flowing white robes and his darkly tanned hands were visible. Occasionally, the glowing light would catch the white orbs of his eyes and flash a piece of humanity to the rest of the room, but those moments were fleeting.

"The information I gave you is absolutely correct," the mysterious man said. His accent was thick, of Arabic descent, though the general had no idea which country he hailed from and honestly didn't care. All he wanted to know was whether the threat had been eliminated. "When you send your teams to the sites, they will find what I told you they will find."

"You sound awfully certain about that," the general sneered. "Didn't you see the footage just now? We reduced every one of those facilities to nothing but rubble and ashes. There won't be much left to find. Convenient, if you ask me."

"He didn't ask you, General," June cut in. "He's been more than helpful with this mission. Red Ring will be significantly weakened after these attacks, if there are any members left at all."

"I'm sorry if I don't share your blind optimism, Ms. Holiday. I suppose I'm not as quick to trust as you are."

"And I'm sorry you think I'm quick to trust. Our source was thoroughly vetted. He was a well-known member of the Red Ring. We've confirmed that through numerous other sources and investigations. Dozens of hours went into verifying the legitimacy of his claims. You know that as well as anyone."

The general shrugged and ticked one of his eyebrows up for a half second. "You can never be too careful, Agent Holiday."

"Yes, sir." She didn't feel like going around and around with this guy.

The general was accustomed to a system littered with red tape. He knew how to navigate it, probably because he was one of those keeping it in place.

June, however, loathed bureaucratic nonsense. It was one of the reasons she'd agreed to work for Shadow Cell and not one of the other agencies in the United States or the UK. She answered to a select few, powerful people, people who trusted her and her team to get the job done at all costs, and by whatever means necessary.

The old Arab in the corner had come to them with vital information, intel that would all but rid the world of the Red Ring, a terrorist organization with more money and weapons than any that had ever been encountered in modern history. Their resources were so vast, their numbers so large, they could field nearly a small army—a formidable force considering no one ever knew their next target. June had no idea about the scope of their reach, how many members had joined, the weapons capabilities they possessed, and the manufacturing volume they controlled.

The old man had confirmed three key targets, none of which Shadow Cell knew about. None of the other big agencies knew about those facilities, either: FBI, CIA, MI5, none of them. The Red Ring was good at keeping secrets, or so it seemed.

June had been beating her head into the same wall over and over again, trying to figure out more about the terrorist organization. After taking out strategic targets, she figured the Red Ring would slink into the shadows for a time. She'd been correct about that. For months, nothing had happened. There were a few bombings from other terrorist cells, but nothing the Red Ring claimed on social media, the internet, or through their radical-leaning broadcast outlet.

Then, out of the blue, the old man emerged from the darkness. He'd been beaten to the point of death. His skin had a dozen cuts in various places from the torture he'd endured at the hands of the Red Ring. According to his story, he was one of the older members of the organization and had questioned the leader's tactics on a certain point, suggesting that they proceed with greater caution, limit their attacks to specific targets, and only at certain times.

His superiors had decried his insolence and punished him accordingly. The physical abuse he endured was nothing compared to what the Red Ring did to his family. The man relayed the story of how he'd been forced to watch his wife and son be executed right before his eyes. Immediately thereafter, the beatings and torture had taken place. All to give him a lesson: never question the leader, a man they called the Teacher.

It was in those moments, he claimed, that he'd realized what the Red Ring really was. They weren't servants of Allah, but monsters, capable of wretched atrocities. The old man relayed a story of how he'd watched the Teacher kill one of his own lieutenants when the man returned from a mission to report what had happened at one of their weapons facilities. The young man had been thrown from a balcony, four stories above the ground. The fall had killed the lieutenant instantly when his skull smacked against the pavement.

Even with all of those gruesome details, June and her friend Adriana Villa hadn't completely trusted the old man's story. Not until he gave them three very specific locations where weapons were being manufactured, stored, and tested.

June ordered three of her best assets, including Adriana, to recon the targets to make sure the man was telling the truth. She'd have bet her entire pension that he was full of it, despite the cuts, bruises, and clear emotional abuse he was displaying.

Then she saw the images, the video, and the specs of all the targets.

The old man hadn't been lying.

Under the cover of darkness, trucks delivered munitions, weapon components, and various other matériel. The number of people in each facility was in the hundreds, and those were just the ones the assets reported. There were likely hundreds more across the globe, perhaps thousands.

June had been point blank when she asked the old man if there were any other facilities. He'd told her there weren't, and the look in his eyes seemed to confirm the truth.

She knew a lie when she saw one. There wasn't one written anywhere on that old man's face.

The scope of a mission like this was too big for her small team of agents. She carried only a handful, ten to be specific. And while all of them were capable of holding their own in the field with a wide array of specialties and skills, taking out all three targets at once was too big a task for her little operation.

She had to call in the big guns, which meant bringing the general on board for one swift-stroke mission.

He'd delivered on his promises, using the latest weapons and tech to eliminate the Red Ring facilities and essentially cripple their ability to harm anyone for a long time, save for the few rogue members of the cell that could venture off on their own.

Now time for him to leave. At least that's how June felt. These types didn't respect what she did or who she was. But she didn't do her job for respect. She did it to protect the free world from tyrants and people who would do them harm.

"Thank you for your help, General. I realize this was a sudden and unexpected use of your valuable time and resources."

Screw his time, she thought. June didn't care if she stole time away from his golf outings or whatever it was he did when he wasn't strutting around in uniform. This guy was a year away from retiring. She half wondered why he hadn't already. He had more than enough years in, which meant—in her mind—that he either liked his job, felt a sense of duty, or was a power junkie. Based on the way he spoke and acted, she leaned toward the latter.

"Yes."

She didn't even get a "you're welcome."

"You'll receive all our findings once we have teams on site to analyze the wreckage. Once those reports are in, I'm sure—"

"Save it, Agent Holiday. I know how these things work. If you're done, I'd like to speak with my men who made all this happen for you. Good day."

He turned on his heel and strode out of the room.

"I bet he's a ton of fun at parties," a new voice said from another corner of the room. Adriana stepped forward from the shadows with arms crossed. Her dark brown hair was pulled back into a tight ponytail. She wore a black tactical jacket, zipped halfway up, with matching cargo pants and black boots. She stopped next to the conference table where two more agents were sitting with laptops open, busily scanning incoming data.

She preferred to stay silent when it came to meetings like this. Adriana learned long ago that action was often better than words, especially when it came to certain kinds of personalities. The general fit into that category. People who had egos the size of skyscrapers didn't want to hear anyone else's opinions on anything. All they wanted was information to make decisions, and then when the choice was made they took all the credit for their brilliant leadership. She snorted at the last thought.

The old man in the corner stood. "Men like him are why men like me did what we did." There was a hint of regret in his voice as well as a hefty helping of disdain.

"We thank you for your cooperation with all this," June said. "I'm truly sorry for his arrogance. He's accustomed to doing things a certain way."

The man waved it off. "I understand completely. Were the situation reversed and one of you had shown up on my doorstep with the kind of information I brought, I would be equally as mistrusting, if not more so."

"I appreciate your understanding. That's still no reason for him to be rude like that."

"I've learned that people will either be rude to your face or stab you in the back. I prefer the former." The dark, weathered face stretched into a grin. The man's teeth flashed brilliant white against his tanned features.

June gave a grateful nod. "Adriana will escort you to your transport. From there, you will be taken to an undisclosed location where you'll be taken care of. You'll have a new life here, and you won't have to worry about the Red Ring anymore. Your identity will be safe."

"Thank you." Tears formed in the corners of his eyes. "I just..." He broke down for a moment, and the two women glanced at each other, their hearts aching for him. "I'm sorry." He wiped one eye with a tissue. "I only wish I could have saved my family. They would have truly loved it here. I suppose, in a way, they have their freedom, too. I will join them someday."

"Don't apologize," Adriana said. "Take as much time as you need. I'll wait out in the hall for you."

The man shook his head. "No." He wiped the other eye clean and stood up a little straighter. "I'm fine. I have mourned them long enough. It's time for me to start living again, if not for myself then for them. I am ready."

Adriana clenched a sympathetic smile. "Right this way then." She motioned toward the door.

They made their way through the brick hallways lit by ancient lights hanging from the ceiling every ten feet. June had relayed the rendezvous point for Adriana to take the informant before the meeting took place. Everything was planned down to the tiniest detail.

The Red Ring, though severely weakened by the attacks on their installations, was still a formidable group. June had specifically left that information out of her report to the general. There was no need to cause him undue concern. On top of that, she didn't fully trust the man. One misstep and he would push the government to shut her agency down, or worse: put it under his control. That was the last thing she wanted.

Shadow Cell operated with remarkable efficiency, partially due to its size. If someone like the general took charge, he would no doubt try to expand operations. That couldn't be allowed. The agents under June's command were fiercely loyal to her, in part due to the fact she'd recruited all of them personally. Adriana was the last addition; the final piece to a fighting machine that could take the battle to evil people without worrying about the confines of what politicians had decided was right or wrong. They were judge, jury, and executioner as far as she was concerned. And she wanted to keep it that way.

A guard pushed open the metal door at the end of the hall as Adriana approached. She gave a curt "thank you" and stepped out into the fresh air. Gray clouds covered the sky from one end of the horizon to the other.

The old man followed her into the dim daylight and looked around, squinting despite the lack of sunshine. It was still brighter than the halls and meeting room they'd just left.

"Right this way, sir." Adriana motioned to a black SUV parked twenty feet away. The driver was already positioned behind the wheel with the engine running. Another guard stood next to the back driver-side door and at the sight of his cargo pulled it open for them.

Once the two were inside, the guard shut the door and climbed into the front. The driver hit the gas immediately and the vehicle sped off, whipping around in a tight U-turn before driving to a fenced gate guarded by two more men with HK-5 submachine guns.

Out on the street, the SUV proceeded quickly, heading for the center of town. No one in the vehicle said a word. They didn't need to. It was a somber moment but also one that required intense focus. The two highly trained soldiers in the front worked for the British government. They took security seriously and had no intention of screwing up this drop-off; and Adriana had no intention of interrupting their focus.

She had her own thoughts to mull over, though she tried to keep her focus on their surroundings as they continued into downtown Liverpool. Still, her thoughts drifted to Sean. She wondered what he was doing, where he was. She imagined he and Tommy had found themselves in no end of trouble since she and June had fallen off the map. There'd been phone calls, occasional text messages or emails, but while in the field and on assignment Adriana knew personal contacts had to be forgotten.

Easier said than done.

The driver slammed on the brakes and sent the vehicle's occupants surging forward. Adriana instinctively stuck out her hand to the left to keep the old man from hurting himself. As their inertia died, she lifted her head to see why the driver had stopped so suddenly.

"My apologies," he said.

Then she saw what caused the halt. A line of protesters marched through the intersection, holding signs, raising fists, and shouting at the top of their lungs.

Adriana frowned. She appreciated people voicing their opinions, just not when it interfered with extremely important business.

She let out a sigh. "Can we get an alternate route?"

"Working on it, Mum," the man in the front passenger seat said.

"The price of free speech," the informant commented with a smile. "Patience, my friends."

That was easy for him to say. Actually, it shouldn't have been easy. He should have been freaking out. At least that's what Adriana was thinking. If she were in his shoes, she'd be antsy and want to get to protected services as quickly as possible.

She craned her neck to the side and looked out through the windshield. Two men in front of the SUV got out of their hatchback and put their hands up, clearly frustrated that they had to wait for the protesters to march by.

Adriana turned around and looked through the back window. Cars were beginning to line up behind them.

She had started to turn back when the old man suddenly swung his arm around and struck her in the throat. Adriana gasped, suddenly unable to get air through her windpipe. Simultaneously, the two men standing next to their car spun around with pistols extended. They opened fire, easily puncturing the windshield with each shot. The old man in the back had already removed his seatbelt and was exiting through the open door, ducking to avoid the flurry of bullets.

The driver and his partner shook violently as each round penetrated their chests, necks and faces. Then, as quickly as it began, the firing ended. The two shooters rushed to the old man and grabbed him as he covered his head with his hands. They ushered him to their car, flung open the back door, and shoved him in. Once he was safely inside, the driver slammed the door shut and jumped in behind the wheel while his partner took a step toward the SUV and slung a courier bag under the engine block.

He hurried back to the open door of his car, climbed in, and the hatchback spun its wheels, slinging the back end around as it did a U-turn and sped away.

In the back of the SUV, Adriana clutched her throat with one hand and the door handle with the other. She pulled on it, but when she tried to get out, she felt the tug around her waist. The seatbelt was still buckled.

Then the street, the terrified protesters, and all the cars around her, blinked into darkness.

2

LIVERPOOL

Adriana blinked her eyes, but the muscles were slower than usual, heavier. The world beyond her eyelids spun in a blurry haze. She heard strange noises, a chaotic jumble of sound, swelling and falling in the midst of a constant ring in her eardrums. Her head hurt, like she'd tried to head butt a ram. She also felt a soreness in her throat and instinctively moved her hand to feel her neck. Her labored breaths came in weary gasps. Then she noticed the smell.

Something familiar and terrifying wafted into her nostrils. Smoke. It was acrid, something she'd smelled many times before. She rubbed her eyes with one hand as she kept blinking, faster and faster. The sounds around her started to separate. Screams of women and children, men yelling, someone crying, and sirens, dozens of sirens, all filtered through her ears and registered in her mind.

Her vision cleared next, the haze quickly fading to a clear view of the world around her, which wasn't much. It was then she realized why her head felt so heavy. She was upside down in the back of an SUV.

She reached for the seatbelt buckle, put a hand on the ceiling below her, and pressed the button. Falling, her shoulders hit with a thud along with the back of her neck and skull. She winced but collected herself enough to scramble onto her backside and sit upright. Why was she upside down?

That question would have to wait.

She needed to get out of here.

Adriana reached out and grasped the door handle and gave it a tug. Luckily, the door swung free and hung open, pulled outward by gravity. She crawled out onto the pavement, eyes locked on the sidewalk. Her muscles pushed hard against the street surface, but when she made it to her feet she tumbled forward as the world began spinning again, tilted on a diagonal axis. She rolled onto the sidewalk and paused for a second, giving herself a break for the briefest of moments. Then she saw the smoldering undercarriage of the SUV.

She frowned as she gazed at the torn pieces of steel plates running from just ahead of the front axle all the way to the concealed fuel tank in the back.

"A bomb?" She said the words out loud, surprised she'd been able to even speak at that point. Her voice was nothing more than a croaky whisper.

The plates under the vehicle had likely saved her life. The driver and the front passenger, she noticed, hadn't been so lucky.

"What happened?" she muttered.

With one hand on the concrete pavement, she propped herself up as an emergency medical technician rushed to her side and started asking her a flurry of questions. She heard some of the words. Others, not so much. She understood enough to tell the EMT she was fine, just shaken up, but he didn't listen. He asked her to lie back down on the ground so he could check her out. While his hands worked fast, going through a rudimentary procedure to make sure she wasn't going to fall over dead, Adriana rolled her head to the side.

Cops flooded the scene, rushing to help those who were hurt and usher people capable of moving away from the area. Firemen sprayed the SUV's undercarriage with a foamy concoction that spread close to where she was lying.

"I told you," she said. "I'm fine. Go help someone else. I'll be okay."

The paramedic looked her in the eyes and then gave a curt nod. "Right," he said in an English accent. "You still need to get out of here and you could have some internal injuries."

"I know what internal injuries feel like," she half lied. "I'm good. Just some bruising. Go."

The man didn't put up another argument. He grabbed his bag and took off toward a cluster of bodies strewn on the pavement. One of them wasn't moving. The others were writhing in agony amid the acrid smoke still lingering above the street.

Adriana rolled over onto her side and pushed herself up onto her elbow. She took a deep breath and then stood up. Her ears were still ringing, and as a result her equilibrium was in a tailspin. The world dipped in front of her at an angle, twisting away at a rapid pace. She closed her eyes, squeezing the lids tight for a moment, and then snapped her head to regain focus.

She'd been dizzy before. This was something else. In an instant, she understood the awful feeling of vertigo and wished it would go away, never to return.

Her eyes opened, and the world wasn't spinning quite so fast. Things were starting to settle in her eardrums, at least that's what she figured, though her medical knowledge was rudimentary at best.

One pervasive thought kept pounding in the back of her head, along with the literal pounding that was sending an ache through her skull: she had to get back to HQ.

Adriana stumbled back down the street, weaving her way through the chaos of first responders, victims, gurneys, and emergency vehicles. She looked like a drunken reveler after ninety minutes in Goodison Park on a Saturday afternoon, wobbling and stumbling as she pushed through toward Shadow Cell headquarters.

Did they even know what happened? For that matter, what had happened?

She neared the perimeter where cops were setting up tape to keep out reporters and onlookers.

She neared a uniformed cop and he glanced at her with wide eyes. "You okay, Miss?"

"I'm fine. Just trying to get out of the way." She managed to get the words out despite feeling like he knew she was lying.

He gave a doubtful nod and lifted the tape so she could walk under without having to bend down too much. Once she was on the other side of the line, the street seemed more chaotic for the first fifty yards. Hundreds of people had gathered to see what was going on.

What were they doing? They should be running as far away from here as possible.

Adriana shook her head at the stupid hive mentality that people possessed when it came to things like this. Just like a car crash on the road, people couldn't help slowing down to take a look at the grisly scene. This one was far worse and would, undoubtedly, make international news in the coming minutes.

The crowd thinned as she kept struggling forward. More police units appeared around the corner, hurrying toward the scene with their sirens blaring. She cupped her ears against the painful sound until the squad cars had passed.

Then she reached the end of the block and looked in the direction of the old brick building she'd left just minutes ago. Was it minutes? She didn't know. Time had slowed down. She might have been unconscious for twenty minutes or an hour, though she doubted it was the latter. First responders weren't that slow.

She took a step forward, confident she could make it back to HQ in short time. Suddenly, a deep boom shook the very ground under her feet. The light post to her right rattled loudly. Car alarms blared.

Then there was a bang. She grabbed at the building's wall next to her to keep her balance as the street shook. The shop sign over her head swung back and forth in huge, dramatic sways. Adriana stepped away from the wall and wrapped her arms around the light pole, thinking it would be safer than potentially being crushed by a store sign.

She narrowed her eyes, gazing toward the HQ building in horror. A massive black cloud erupted from the area, churning into the sky.

Adriana shook off her aches and pains, pushed the dizziness aside, and started toward the smoke.

Her feet danced back and forth, uncoordinated as she jogged ahead. More sirens screamed in the distance. Various alarms mixed in with the anarchy, along with more screams from the people on the streets and sidewalks.

The journey back to the warehouse entrance took more minutes than it should have, but she wasn't feeling 100 percent. When she finally reached it, what she discovered sent a chill through her body, then a terrible ache, and then a flood of emotions.

Adriana dropped to her knees, tears streaming down her face to mix with the black-and-red smears of burned residue and blood. She bent over, feeling bile rising in the back of her throat, desperate to push its way out of her mouth.

She choked it down but heaved a couple of times anyway. Tears dripped onto the sidewalk, puddling with droplets of blood that were falling from some unseen cut on her face or head.

Then Adriana straightened herself up and looked at the scene before her once more. She screamed at the top of her lungs with a haunting yell that could have frightened the most hardened soldier.

A few hundred yards away, the building that housed Shadow Cell's headquarters was gone, consumed by raging fires and roiling gray-and-black smoke.

Adriana's breath came faster. Her chest rose and fell quickly. The scene before her began to spin again, and she felt something she'd not felt in a long time. It was a tingling in her body. The sound of sand pouring in an hourglass filled her ears. She knew what was coming and lay down on the concrete to keep from doing more damage to herself.

She welcomed the unconsciousness. It was better than facing the reality that existed just across the gravel parking lot.

Everyone in Shadow Cell HQ was dead.

3

LIVERPOOL

Adriana's head rolled to the side. The sudden dropping motion caused her to wake, and she blinked her eyes in rapid succession, attempting to get her bearings.

She came out of the swirling pink haze to a world unlike anything she'd ever seen. People were rushing around inside a hospital hallway. There were patients on gurneys lining the walls, leaving only a narrow thoroughfare in the center for medical workers to pass.

She twisted her neck, and her head rolled back, sinking into a thin hospital pillow. She breathed slowly at first as her senses began to bounce back. First to recover was the feeling in her fingertips and toes. Smells were there from the beginning, filling her nose with the sterile smell of hospital cleaners.

What was going on?

She kept the question to herself, not wishing to garner any more attention. A quick shift of her hands, and she was able to prop herself up on the narrow bed and get a better look around.

Victims. That was the first thing she realized. All these people were victims?

The triage setup in the hospital corridor must have been thrown together on the fly. Why? What had happened?

She sighed as the memory returned. The bombing. There'd been an attack on her car. The two men in front were killed by a couple of gunmen. That much she remembered. The rest was a little hazy. She'd crawled out of the SUV, as evidenced by some minor scraps on her elbows and knees. Then what?

Right. She'd walked back to HQ just in time to...

A lump of bile rose in her throat, and she craned her neck to the side in case she threw up. Somehow, she managed to keep it down and returned to her upright position.

Someone had blown up the Shadow Cell headquarters, likely killing anyone remaining inside. Her thoughts drifted to June, and a dagger shot through her chest, digging into her heart with a sickening pain. She'd been in the building when Adriana left. She was likely still there when the devastating bomb leveled the building.

Adriana continued to take in the scene before her. It was unlike anything she'd seen in a hospital before. She'd spent her fair share of time in those places while her mother was suffering; fighting a losing battle against a cancer that wouldn't be beaten.

A child cried down the hall, snapping Adriana's attention back to the moment. The kid was screaming for their mother. Adriana frowned then grimaced as she swung her legs over the edge of the rolling bed. Her head wasn't hurting anymore. That was a plus. And her ears? The ringing was gone.

She vaguely recalled having a pounding headache and a bad case of tinnitus while she was on the street. From the looks of things, that wasn't long ago. How she'd ended up in the hospital was a mystery, though she figured some emergency personnel had loaded her into an ambulance and dropped her off.

The kid screamed again from somewhere to the left. Adriana craned her neck out over the floor to see if she could find them, but there wasn't a child in sight. That didn't mean much. The hallway was packed with people, overflowing from one end to the other. A small child would be difficult to spot.

Adriana let her feet dangle for a moment. She glanced down at her wrists where something was causing it to itch. Someone had started an IV on her. It was hooked to an empty bag hanging from a hook nearby. There was a wristband on the other arm for identification purposes, but the name was blank. Only a bar code was printed on it to keep track of the medications she'd been given.

She reached down and fiddled with the tube for a moment when a voice interrupted her.

"Hey, don't mess with that." She lifted her head to meet the irritated gaze of a man in blue scrubs, a white lab coat, and a good amount of sweat. Wire-framed glasses perched atop his nose. His short, thinning red hair parted in the center, revealing the freckled, pale scalp.

She glared at him. "Get me out of this thing."

He took a step toward her, pulled a chart out of the end of the bed, and glanced at it. He looked up once more into her rich brown eyes. "No name?"

"I like to keep some things secret." She took another look around, gathering the visual information surrounding her. "Who are all these people? Why are they here?"

He shrugged off the comment. "Bombings. Three on the street. One in an old warehouse. Miss, you were found unconscious outside the warehouse explosion earlier this afternoon. We're working hard right now to make sure the most desperate of the patients receive care, but you can't leave. Based on this, you probably need to stay here tonight for observation."

His sharp English accent was charming and irritating at the same time. The irritation, she knew, stemmed from the fact that he seemed unwilling to give her what she wanted.

"Fine," she said. "I'll take it out myself."

She reached down to remove the needle, but he stepped closer, putting out his hand to protest. "Wait. Wait. I don't have time for this. Whatever. Here."

He tinkered with the line for a second and then withdrew the needle. Then he reached over to the wall where some shelves contained gauze and other first-aid items. Deftly, he shoved the gauze packet into his mouth, tore it open with one hand while gripping the other end with his teeth. He shoved the fabric over the place where the needle was sticking into her skin and then pulled it out.

She didn't even wince.

"Keep pressure on that for a second," he ordered, reaching for a roll of tape behind her. She did as told while he took a strip of tape and placed it over the gauze.

"There," he said. "Go nuts. I have other people to see."

She gave an appreciative nod and watched the doctor scurry away into the melee.

Adriana still heard the crying and turned toward it. She had pressing issues, like who in the world had caused all this? That question would have to wait. There were other, more immediate ones that needed answering.

She sighed, still hearing the little boy's voice in her ears, and headed down the hall toward the sound. She made her way past a woman with an oxygen mask on. Her body was covered in a blanket, but her face looked like she'd been beaten with a baseball bat—by the entire 1961 New York Yankees team. The skin was swollen and purple. A cut had been closed over her right eye by one of the emergency personnel. She was alive, but the woman would be sore.

Adriana passed a mirror on the wall and caught a glimpse of her reflection. Her hair was matted in one spot on the right side of her head. The rest was a tangled mess. A thin cut on her cheek and a few bloody smears mingled with some black residue, but other than that she looked okay.

Her head snapped back to the right, and she caught a glimpse of a little boy standing against the wall between two empty gurneys. Adriana checked both directions and then moved close to the boy, putting her hand on his shoulder with a gentle, motherly touch.

"What's the matter?" she asked. She didn't have much experience with children. Never really wanted any of her own. That didn't mean she didn't like them or care about them. Kids were the last piece of innocence left in a world that seemed to be growing more corrupt, more evil every day.

"My mommy," was all the boy could manage through his choking sobs.

Adriana looked into his red, tear-filled eyes. "Where is your mommy? When did you see her last?"

He coughed for a few seconds and then wiped his eyes. "On the street." The kid pointed down the hall in the direction of the exit.

"So, you lost her on the street?"

He nodded with a whimpering, "Mmm-hmm."

"Okay, what does she look like? Does she look like me?"

He cracked a smile. "No." He shook his head dramatically.

Adriana knew the kid would think that funny. He had pale skin with red hair. Her dark features framed a midland Spanish tan.

"No, of course not. How silly of me." She offered him a playful smile. "So, what color is her hair? Is it yellow, black, brown, or red?"

He swallowed hard, trying to keep his composure.

Brave little fellow, she thought.

"Yellow."

"Okay then. So, we're looking for a lady with yellow hair. Is she pretty?"

The boy grinned and nodded eagerly.

"All right then. Would you like to stay here while I look for her, or do you want to come with me?"

He bit his lower lip as it quivered. She already knew the answer. With a sigh, she reached out her hand for him. He took it and held on to three of her fingers.

"Okay, but stay close. It's a little crazy in here right now."

He squeezed her hand tighter.

Adriana led the boy through the maze of people, rolling beds, and clutter that filled the corridor. She had no idea how she was going to find the boy's mother in all this. Then there was the other possibility, the worst-case scenario. What if the woman was dead?

"The last place you saw her was on the street, right?"

The boy nodded.

"Okay. Which street? Was it outside the hospital?"

He shook his head.

She gave an understanding nod as they neared the exit. The double doors burst open as a gurney rumbled in, pushed by a redheaded woman in a lab coat, escorted by a younger man with thick, curly black hair and skin like mocha. He was administering oxygen, moving sideways as the bed rolled through the center of the hall.

Adriana yanked the boy back against the wall with her to let the gurney pass and then looked back as they turned into another set of doors leading into an operating room.

She clenched her jaw. So many people had been affected by this, whatever this was. A pair of words kept rising in the back of her mind: *terrorist attack*.

Her eyes drifted back down to the little boy, and she urged him on. "Come. Let's get outside and see if we can find your mama."

He put on his best courageous face and followed her out the doors into the front of the hospital.

Six ambulances were parked in the front. One of them switched on its emergency lights, blipped the siren, and accelerated back out onto the road. Cops were out in the street directing traffic, doing their best to keep ordinary citizens off the streets to make way for the constant flow of emergency vehicles.

Adriana pulled the boy off to the side to keep the path clear for more EMTs bringing people in on rolling stretchers.

"You said that you lost her somewhere else, right?"

The boy nodded. "How did you get here?"

"The policeman brought me." His voice was still between sobs and cracking.

That didn't narrow it down. There were probably three dozen cops in the area, and that was just outside the building. Still more were likely at the scene of the explosions.

The explosions. The thought brought everything back to Adriana's mind. The gunmen that had turned on their SUV and killed the driver and front-seat passenger.

She shook her head to free herself of the thoughts. Those things had to wait. Right now, she needed to get this kid to his mom.

Adriana turned her head back and forth, scanning the area for anyone who looked like they were coordinating the chaos.

She found her guy about twenty feet away. He was in a button-up shirt with a badge dangling from a black lanyard around his neck. From the hand gestures alone, Adriana could tell this guy was some kind of crisis management official, though his actual title could have been anything.

"Come on." She realized she didn't know the boy's name. "What's your name?"

"George," the boy said. "My name is George."

"Named after your mom and dad's favorite football player?"

The boy beamed. "Yeah. How did you know?"

Adriana knew more than her fair share about top-level European soccer, or football as she and the rest of the world called it. She and her boyfriend, Sean, had enjoyed many short discussions on that topic.

"Lucky guess," she said. "Come on. Let's see if that man over there has seen your mother."

Adriana led the boy across the looped asphalt in front of the emergency room and stopped short of the guy. He was shouting commands to incoming medical personnel and other workers, trying to keep everything running smoothly and efficiently. She didn't want to imagine what it might have looked like if he wasn't there.

"Excuse me, sir," she said.

He snapped his head around and looked at her with surprise. Then he turned and issued another order to a nurse pushing another wheeled stretcher into the hospital.

"Yes?" His response was short and sharp, though Adriana knew he meant nothing by it.

"This boy," she said, "he was brought here by a police officer earlier, but he and his mom were separated, and he doesn't know where she is."

The intense look of stress and worry melted on the man's face as he looked down into the little boy's eyes.

"What did your mom look like, young man?"

"She's blonde. He says she's pretty."

George nodded.

"Blonde, pretty lady. We've had several females brought in that could fit that description. Was she hurt?"

George gave another nod. "There was a bump on her head and a cut on her arm."

That was more information than the boy had given Adriana during her initial interrogation, though to be fair, she'd not dug that deep. In hindsight, that should have been at the top of her list of queries.

The man twisted his head and motioned for another group of people to keep moving. Some were workers. Others were just standing around, gawking at the scene.

He pulled up a radio he'd been holding in his hand and pressed the button. "Hey, I'm looking for a blonde woman, well-kept, came in probably the last hour or so with a knock to the head and a cut on one arm. Anyone know where she might be?"

He released the button and waited for a second.

Twenty seconds went by, and he raised the radio to speak again in case no one heard his initial question.

"Yeah," a voice came through the speaker. "Second floor. Came in just over an hour ago. Been hysterical. Said she needs her son."

George's eyes widened.

"Room number?"

"Yeah, she's in 238."

"Thanks. Out."

He lowered his radio. "Room 238, ma'am."

He spun around and started barking orders again to get the roundabout cleared. Sirens screamed in the distance, bearing down on the hospital.

"Thank you," Adriana said and ushered the boy away.

They worked their way through the anarchy once more until they found the elevators and managed to squeeze their way in. Adriana was a little surprised the lifts were working considering the scope of how many people were being treated at the time.

The hospital was on overload, and she knew many victims were likely being transferred to other hospitals or even to other regions.

On the second floor the elevator dinged, and the doors opened to a slightly less but still chaotic scene. There weren't as many beds parked in the halls, but medical workers were rushing around at a furious pace.

Adriana stepped out onto the floor with George at her side, still holding her hand.

She glanced around and found what she was looking for to her left. A sign displayed which rooms were in which direction. Room 238 fell between a set of numbers that were straight ahead.

"Come on, George. Let's find your mom."

The two made their way down the hall, Adriana checking each room number they passed to make sure they were going the right direction. She hoped that the boy's mom was okay, although if something had happened to her to cause her condition to worsen, they wouldn't be keeping her in a room.

She was one of the lucky ones, not just because she was alive but because she was in a room. The poor souls downstairs were still waiting.

"There it is," George said, pointing at the placard next to a door that was cracked open.

"Smart boy," Adriana whispered.

George let go of her hand and rushed toward the door before Adriana could stop him. He barged through it to find a doctor holding a chart next to a bed. A blonde woman with tubes in one arm and a purple bruise on her forehead was propped up with tears streaming down her face.

"Mommy!" the boy shouted as he rushed toward her.

"Georgie?" The mom's tears of grief and panic turned to ones of joy and relief. "Georgie! My boy! Oh, I'd thought I'd lost you!"

George ran to his mother's side and hugged her leg.

"Easy, young man," the doctor in the lab coat said. His glasses slid down a long beak of a nose. He had thin gray hair like a nest on top of his head. "She's had a rough day, but she's going to be fine."

Adriana stood in the doorway for a second, taking in the heart-warming scene.

"How on earth did you find me in all this mess, Georgie?"

His mother ran her fingers through his hair, tousling it.

George turned and pointed to the door. "The lady. She helped me."

The doorway was empty.

The boy frowned and cocked his head to the side. "Where did she go?"

Adriana was already to the stairs by the time George reached the empty door and poked his head out to find her.

One mission complete.

Now it was time to find the people responsible for this.

4

LIVERPOOL

Adriana trudged down the sidewalk, barely able to lift her feet off the ground, her shoes scuffing the concrete along the way.

She had no idea where she was going, what to do, or what was going to happen next. She simply kept picking up one foot after the other, moving away from the hospital through the canyons of shops, pubs, and businesses. Taller structures loomed a dozen blocks away, the epicenter of downtown where the old mercantile city had given rise to more modern bastions of trade and commerce. There were still some of the famous, older buildings. The most prominent were known as the Three Graces: the Royal Liver Building, the Cunard Building, and the Port of Liverpool Building on the pier head.

Adriana's mind swirled with more thoughts than she could contain. She'd been lucky to survive; that much she knew for certain. Her foot caught on a crack in the sidewalk and she tripped, stumbling forward and almost running into a fish-and-chips cart. Tragedy, it seemed, didn't mean there wasn't an opportunity for entrepreneurship.

People had to eat, she figured.

She navigated around the cart with its deep-fried aromas spilling out in huge clouds of steam, and kept moving.

"Okay, focus," she said to herself. "What happened?"

It was the first question she wanted...no, needed to answer. The events from earlier in the day ran through her head.

"There was a parade," she said, ignoring the looks she got from some of the people hurrying by on their way to the hospital. "A protest or something."

She reached the end of the street and turned left, heading down a corridor filled with pubs and restaurants. She considered going in to a tavern on the corner but decided she should keep moving.

"Then the men in the car in front of us turned and opened fire." She winced at the memory, cursing herself for not seeing the ambush coming. Then again, the two dead men in the front of the SUV should have seen it, too. They hadn't been amateurs.

Adriana blinked rapidly, trying to remember what happened next. The explosion had occurred shortly after the shooting. Then it hit her.

The gunmen had taken the old man, their witness. The fog in her head started to clear as she recalled the moment the old man got out of the car. Adriana's face curled in confusion; a fleeting glimpse, a mere second that stood out in her mind's eye. She'd not remembered it before, not in all the chaos.

Now, though, that second in time punched her in the chest like a howitzer.

The old man.

He hadn't panicked during the ambush. He didn't even look concerned. His eyes flashed in her memory, a look he'd given as he exited the SUV mere moments before the bomb flipped the vehicle and her life onto its head.

It wasn't a kidnapping. It was an extraction.

She swore in Spanish under her breath and stopped in the middle of the sidewalk. Then she spun around, making sure no one was following her.

"Think, Adriana," she said to herself. "What are you going to do?"

Shadow Cell was an ultra-secret agency. They were, for the most part, off the books. She didn't know who knew about them and who didn't. The prime minister knew, but he would be untouchable at this point. The media would call this a terrorist attack, which meant government officials would be under even more intense security during the coming weeks. Everything would be heightened, and the leader of the United Kingdom would be impossible to reach.

Then there was the little matter of having no contacts. She'd been isolated, and that fact loomed heavy in her mind now. Her primary point of communication had been June. Other than that, Adriana didn't have many—if any—resources. Her cell phone bulged in her front left pocket, but she felt like the device was almost useless at this point. She could call Sean and probably needed to. Something inside her, though, told her not to. Why? He could help. He might even be closer than she realized. His job with the International Archaeological Agency took him all over the world. It was entirely possible he was in England at this very moment.

The little independent voice in the back of her head begged her not to call him. She could handle this herself. She was no damsel in distress. Well, the distress part was true enough, but she could handle herself.

I need answers. Who to call?

The thought of her friend brought back a hurricane of emotions that punched her square in the gut, and she nearly slapped herself in the face to keep from crying. There would be a time to mourn later. Right now, she needed solutions. She stopped again and stuck her hand into her pocket. Maybe she wasn't without *all* her resources.

Sure enough, she found her identification, room key, and a credit card held together with a rubber band. Normally, these would have been kept in her hotel room, except for the room key. That day, however, she'd brought them with her.

That meant she had money and a way to travel. Her passports, both real and fake, were back in the room, which also meant she could go pretty much wherever she needed. A faint flicker of hope rose inside her.

Now the problem was where to go next.

The hotel room was the obvious answer. Then again, there was the concern that she'd be walking into a trap, another ambush. The men that attacked her SUV and bombed Shadow Cell HQ could easily be there waiting. She dismissed that with a shake of the head.

No one would be there. She didn't have anything worth stealing other than a laptop, some petty cash, and a few personal belongings.

That settled it. Back to the hotel.

Adriana pulled out her phone and was relieved to see it still had some battery life left. A few taps of her thumbs, and she pulled up her rideshare app to call a car. She was about to press the confirm button when she stopped with her thumb hanging over the screen.

She suddenly closed the app and stuffed the phone back in her pocket, paranoid that someone might be tracking her.

She saw a black cab rolling down the street in her direction and stuck out her hand to hail the driver. It was one of those traditional-style vehicles that looked like it was something out of a 1960s spy movie. The body lines were curved and dramatic. The flat windshield sat within a tall frame that made the vehicle look like the least wind resistant car in the world.

The driver stopped next to the curb, and Adriana climbed in, gave him the name of the hotel, and dug the phone out of her pocket again.

She wasn't going to call Sean. Not yet. As far as he was concerned, he didn't know what she was up to and where she was, so he wouldn't be worried about her safety. Why would she be in Liverpool?

A sigh escaped her lips. Tommy, on the other hand, would eventually have to be told what happened to June. Her heart that ached so much for her own loss now hurt for his. She knew how he felt about her. Those emotions pumped more fuel into a single line of thought that burned like an inferno inside her.

She had to make those responsible for this pay for what they did.

The cab driver stopped the car outside her hotel. She quickly scanned the card reader in the back, gave him a generous tip as well as a thank-you, and then climbed out.

The scene at the hotel couldn't have been more opposite of the streets she'd left just minutes before. It was almost as if nothing had happened.

The doorman stood outside the brass double doors that framed huge panes of glass. He looked bored. Pedestrians strolled by, most discussing the terrorist attack that had rocked the entire city and probably the world.

Adriana strode across the sidewalk to the entrance. There was a pain in her left thigh, but she winced and did her best to ignore it. Probably a bruise; at least that's what she figured. She'd been banged up before. It wouldn't be the last time. She'd grown up a little rough and tumble. That's how her father had wanted it. He believed Adriana needed to be strong and independent, able to take care of herself no matter the circumstances.

He'd spent time training her as best he could until her skills surpassed his own. Then he'd hired some of the best in Europe to teach her the arts of hand-to-hand combat, survival, and weaponry.

She'd learned four foreign languages, including English, by the time she was eleven, adding two more before her sixteenth birthday.

Despite the intense training and the lifelong learning, nothing could have prepared her for the suffering and death her mother endured at the hands of cancer. It was, in a strange way, the final piece of her warrior's journey, the last test of her strength and character.

Adriana stepped through the doorway and into the hotel, making her way quickly across the lobby floor until she reached the elevator. She was well aware of her appearance, probably too much so. She felt like every eye in the building was staring at her. In truth, few people except the hotel workers even noticed her. Everyone was so preoccupied with the attack that they didn't give her a second glance. Even the concierge barely looked her way.

Inside the elevator, she pressed the button for her floor and waited patiently as the doors closed and the lift took her up. When the doors opened, she held her breath, thinking momentarily that she'd made a mistake getting on the elevator. She should have taken the stairs. An empty corridor beyond filled her with relief and calmed her nerves.

"Get a hold of yourself, Adriana," she whispered.

She glanced down at her hands. They were still steady, always steady. She'd learned how to keep them that way long ago during her training. She'd only been a young girl when her father put a pistol in her hand. She'd been excited and nervous that day. Guns were scary to her at first, but her father explained that guns weren't meant to be swords. They were tools, used only when necessary and with the greatest of care, like a scalpel.

Adriana grinned at the memory of what she'd said next.

"What's a scalpel, Papa?" The young girl had been full of wonder.

He'd explained the purpose of the surgical instrument and how it was used to remove bad things.

Her first shots at the practice range had been clumsy and wildly inaccurate. It was that day that Diego Villa, her father, taught her how to calm her nerves, to let go of her worries, and to focus on something soothing.

Before she knew it, the shaking hands were gone, replaced by stone.

She moved out of the elevator and into the hallway, faster now. The soreness in her leg dissipated with each step. Her head was feeling better. They must have given her some kind of pain medication at the hospital, though it couldn't have been anything too strong. She still had her wits about her and was thinking clearer now than she had been since the attack.

At the end of the corridor, she rounded the corner to the right and stopped two doors down. A quick swipe of her key card caused the little light on the lock to flash green, and she pulled on the latch.

Adriana hesitated for a second, still unsure if there could be danger lurking on the other side of the door. Then she pushed it open and stepped inside.

The hotel room was dark, the curtains pulled shut. She frowned, trying to remember if she'd left them that way or not. The bathroom to the right was also dark, though the towels had been replaced.

Housekeeping must have come by at some point. Maybe they were the ones who drew the curtains.

She let the door shut loudly behind her and moved farther into the room. As she rounded the corner of the lavish suite, she was hit with the overwhelming feeling that she wasn't alone. Instinctively, she reached for the weapon at her side that wasn't there.

She cursed herself but again tried to calm the anxiety in the back of her mind.

Adriana turned to her left and flipped on a light switch she remembered being there before. When she turned her head back into the small living room, her tanned face flushed pale. Her eyes gaped open in disbelief.

"Adriana. I'm so glad you're okay."

Sitting in a chair in the corner with a pistol across her lap, one hand gripping it tightly, was June Holiday.

5

LIVERPOOL

A wave of dizziness hit Adriana in an instant. She frowned at first, then let out a gasp. *Could this really be June?*

Her friend looked no worse for wear than earlier that morning. June was still dressed in the same outfit as before, her hair still neatly pulled back in a ponytail. Her face was clean and her makeup unmarred.

Adriana swallowed hard and skirted around the edge of the couch, slumping down into the soft cushions. "You're...alive?"

June leaned forward and set the pistol on the coffee table between them. "Sorry for the gun," she said. "I didn't know who would try coming here, if anyone."

Adriana wanted to express that she'd had the same concern, but instead a different word came out. "How?"

June's right eyebrow flicked up, and then she eased back into her seat. "How am I still alive?"

Adriana nodded.

"I'd suggest you take a shower and get cleaned first, then we could talk, but I know you better than that. You want answers now, shower later."

Another nod.

"I, along with two members from my team, followed the general out of the building. We were already miles away when the blast occurred. I had another meeting to attend in London and was on the way to the airport."

"That was lucky," Adriana managed. It was all she could think of.

"Yes. We were fortunate." A twinge of guilt littered her voice. "We lost some good people today, but it could have been far worse. After the aerial strike against the Red Ring targets, most of the building was empty. Two analysts were killed in the blast, as far as I know. Search and rescue are still looking through the rubble, but I know what they'll find. No way those two could have survived."

"I don't understand," Adriana said, her voice trailing off. "How did this happen?"

"The best I can figure is that our snitch was responsible. I heard what happened to your ride, along with our men in the front seat."

"It was all a setup."

June gave a confirming nod. "That's the only explanation that makes sense." There was a hint of regret. "We vetted that old man thoroughly, checked his background, everything. All of it came out clean. I should have been concerned about that."

"About what?"

"About how clean it actually was. It was too clean. No one has a spotless record. This guy didn't even have a parking ticket."

"Maybe he doesn't drive." Adriana tried to be funny, but it came out as more cynical than anything.

"Either way, I should have realized something fishy was going on. Now four people are dead as a result."

"Like you said, it could have been much worse."

June shook her head. "I put you in harm's way. You're lucky you're not dead."

That much was true. The gunfire, the explosion, the SUV flipping onto its top, any of those things could have snuffed out her life, but they hadn't. She was still here. And as Adriana gazed across the room at her friend, relief began to fill her soul.

"You have no idea," Adriana muttered.

June waited for a few seconds before she asked her next question. "Can you...tell me what happened?"

Another swallow caught in Adriana's throat. "Yeah." She rubbed the back of her head where it had been throbbing before. Now it was only sore but a reminder of what had occurred. "There was a protest or a parade or something. The street was blocked. As we sat there waiting for the procession to clear, two men in front of us were standing outside their car. At first, I thought they were watching the parade. Then they spun around and opened fire. The driver and other guy in the front were killed quickly. I saw what was happening and ducked down. Instincts, I guess."

More memories ripped through her mind: the sound of gunfire, bullets tearing through leather and cushions, glass shattering.

"The old man got out of the car. Actually, they got him out. I wondered if it was a hit on him. You know? Like they were coming to get him to make him pay for what he'd done."

"A rival extremist group exacting revenge." June cocked her head to the side.

"Yeah, but it was too quick for that. Too soon after the bombings."

"Agreed."

"It was an extraction. That was the only thing that made sense. The entire operation was a sham, a ruse. Have your people searched the targets yet?"

June crossed one leg over the other knee, folding her hands together in her lap. She looked the image of professional composure. "They're en route, but I have a bad feeling they won't find anything. Sure, the Red Ring may have left a few traces of chemical weapons or other dangerous materials lying around, but based on the events of today and what you're telling me, I'd wager those locations were mostly empty."

Adriana knew she was right. It was what she'd been thinking as well. They'd been duped, roped in by an artist.

"Does the general know about all this?" Adriana asked.

"Everyone knows about the attacks," June said. "It's all over the news, from the States to Tokyo and everywhere in between. But that's not what you meant."

Adriana twisted her head once to confirm her friend's assessment.

"As far as our informant, no. He has no idea that the man escaped or that he's even missing yet. There's too much going on for him to worry with that. Not to mention that national security is his primary concern at the moment. It will be days, maybe even a week before he starts poking his nose into that question."

"And you'll tell him what?"

"The easiest line is to let him believe what he wants to believe. He likely thinks that this was the work of a rival terrorist cell or at best, one that was working with the Red Ring. I'm fine with letting him continue to think that for as long as he wants."

A chuckle escaped Adriana's lips in the form of two snorts.

June smiled, then her face grew serious. "I'm glad you're okay. Do you need anything? You hurting?"

"Nothing a few ibuprofen can't fix," Adriana said, dismissing her friend's concern. "I've been through worse." She sighed. "They slid a bomb under the SUV. Blew the thing onto its roof. When I came around, I was hanging from my seatbelt. I managed to climb out. An emergency medical tech looked at me, but I told them to go help someone else. I managed to crawl away from the wreckage and get to my feet, although that was a struggle, too. I made it back to headquarters just seconds before the building blew." The last words hung in the room for a moment. "Next thing I recall, I woke up in the hospital. It was anarchy in there. Wounded people were lining the halls in beds. It was like a MASH unit."

"And then you came here. Smart."

"It's the only place I *could* go. I thought you and everyone else died inside the building when it blew."

"I was hoping you'd come here. I told myself I'd wait for a day. Some of my people are out checking the hospitals and morgues, but I'll call them off when you get in the shower."

"How was the Red Ring capable of this?"

Adriana's question was blunt yet powerful. It was one that June had been considering for hours.

"The only answer is that we had a leak, someone on the inside. Our security measures are better than almost any in the world. The fact that someone was able to get enough explosives in there to bring down the entire facility...it had to be an inside job."

"Maybe."

June pinched her eyebrows together. "What do you mean? You disagree?"

"No, I'm not saying you're wrong. Check the structure of the building, the design. Was there a flaw of some kind to it? I mean, it *was* a really old building. If the Red Ring knew we were there and there was, say, an old sewer system or a bunch of tunnels underneath, they could have gotten in there."

"There are...were tunnels under it, but we had measures in place to make sure they were secure."

"Not secure enough."

"Indeed."

"When I saw the building blow, the explosion came from below the ground and shot up. It wasn't on the main floor. They knew about the underground rooms and corridors where most of our work took place. The building was basically a bunker with a steel and brick umbrella over top. No, they took it out from underneath. That means they got in through those tunnels."

Adriana was glad to have at least one answer, though how the terrorists got in there was another matter entirely.

"Okay," June relented. "They got in through the tunnels. That still doesn't explain how they knew about us or what we were doing. There are people with high clearance levels who don't know who we are and what we do. That's kind of our thing."

"It was simple," Adriana said, realizing it for the first time. "The old man put out feelers until he got a bite. He knew we were looking for them, for him. So, he did the one thing none of us expected. He turned himself over to us with the idea he could give us strategic targets. We never realized that he was setting a trap."

It made sense, and June knew it. She swore under her breath. "We need to find out who he is."

Adriana snorted another laugh. "We know who he is."

June's frown deepened. "We do?"

"Yes," Adriana said with a nod. "He's their leader, the one they call the Teacher."

June waved a dismissive hand and uncrossed her legs. She stood up and paced over to a bar where three bottles sat in front of two cocktail glasses. She opened up the bottle of whiskey and poured herself a drink, offering Adriana one by holding the bottle in her direction. Adriana declined with a wave of the hand.

June took a sip and then returned to her seat, drink held firmly in her fingers. "You're good, Adriana. Very good. But terrorist leaders don't think that way. And they certainly don't operate that way. They're, for the most part, extraordinary cowards."

Adriana knew that. She was still fairly new at this game, but she'd seen enough evidence over the years that corroborated what June was saying. Most terrorist leaders hid in bunkers or caves, sometimes in urban hideouts far away from prying eyes or cameras that could track them or pinpoint their whereabouts. They preached sacrifice and the honor of dying for the cause, yet when it came down to brass tacks, they often shrank back into the shadows.

She was certain they justified it to their legions of followers in some twisted way. She envisioned some grand speech to that effect, telling their disciples that the movement must continue or something like that. Without a great leader, that couldn't happen. Hordes of people bought it, too. She knew that much. It was just like all the big cults that had cropped up over the last century, promising paradise, a better world, a planet free from evil or nonbelievers. Then when it came time for the ultimate sacrifice, the leaders of those cults were nowhere to be found, or were too afraid to come out of hiding and take the fight into their own hands.

All of that made what this Teacher did so much more powerful.

"That's the genius behind what he did," Adriana said, her voice barely above a whisper. "No other extremist leader went to that length before. He did it. And he pulled it off. Now, wherever he is, he will be revered as a hero, as a commander who was unafraid to take the fight to the enemy. I imagine many will flock to his banner now. Some might even consider him to be some kind of holy figure."

June blinked rapidly as her friend finished. She hadn't thought of that. All this time, they operated under the same presumptions, the same thought processes. It was how battles were won, after all. You identified an enemy's tendencies, their way of doing things, and then you shut it down. Understanding battle tactics was key. It always had been. It's how wars were won.

Then again, wars were also won by underdogs when they broke those tendencies and tried something out of the ordinary, something different.

June recalled her studies of American wars, how the United States gained its freedom in the Revolution by using less-standard tactics and more guerrilla warfare, hit-and-run strategies, and sabotage. The American Civil War was one that should have ended in months, but due to the brilliant and unconventional strategies of Southern generals, that war raged for four years.

Had the Teacher done the unexpected, knowing full well that if he succeeded he would become the stuff of legend and thereby increase his flocks as well as bolstering his cause?

Now that she thought about it, June didn't see that it could be any other way. It had been a deliberate and bold move by the Teacher. And because of it, things were likely going to get a lot more difficult as well as more dangerous.

"We have to find him," June said.

"That's a given. Any idea where he went?"

"Not a clue." She thought for a moment before speaking again. "We'll need to check the footage of all the street cameras where you were attacked. Then we'll have to get footage from the airports in the area."

"Airports?"

June nodded. "All of them. I'm talking Edinburgh, Dublin, Heathrow, Paris, and every little airport between. Anything and everything within driving range. It's unlikely they went to France, but Interpol owes me a favor. I'll get them on it. If this guy took a plane somewhere, I want to know where he took off and where he landed. We figure that out, we can start to isolate his location."

"Sounds like a big operation." Adriana gazed at her friend from across the room. She admired June. The woman was relentless, and once her sights were set on something, there was no stopping her.

"We have to cast a wide net at first. Just like we always do. Eventually, one of the fishes we catch will be the right one."

"Or it will be a fish that knows the fish we're looking for."

"Right."

There was something else weighing heavily on Adriana's mind. She'd not said anything yet because focusing on finding the man responsible for today's attacks was paramount. Now, however, she felt like she had to say what had been on her mind.

"Once we catch him...I don't know if I want to keep doing this."

The comment caught June off guard, but she didn't give a knee-jerk reaction. "That's understandable. I brought you in to this to help us put down a serious threat and to help humanity. If you feel like you've done that when we catch this guy, I won't hold that against you." She leaned forward. "You've become a trusted friend. I know that fighting against evil like this is taxing. It's why Sean wanted out of Axis, why he got out. Honestly, there are days when I don't want to do this anymore, but I know that this job is a blessing and a curse, and I'm the best suited to do it, at least for now. When we catch the Teacher and put an end to the Red Ring, I won't try to keep you on. Okay?"

Adriana let a weak smile cross her lips. "Okay. Then let's find this guy."

6

UZBEKISTAN

The white Mercedes SUV pulled into the front of the building and came to a stop behind two other matching vehicles. Two more parked behind it. The dark-tinted windows gave no clue as to who was inside.

You could never be too careful, even in your own back yard.

A darkly tanned man in the front climbed out wearing black tactical gear. His thick, black eyebrows poked out over top of aviator sunglasses, and he swept the area with a rapid turn of the head. Not that he needed to. They were within a secure zone now. He was a pro, however, as was everyone in that unit. A handful of other similarly dressed soldiers hopped out of the SUVs and formed a perimeter around the central vehicle.

Once everyone was in place, the first guard reached for the back passenger-side door and pulled it open. An older man inside winced at the bright sunlight, pulling his black hood down an inch or two to give him the slightest amount of shade. He'd grown up in this region, spent years in the deserts of the Middle East. It was rare for him to wear sunglasses. Through the course of his life, he'd gotten used to the bright sunshine. Today, he didn't want to blot out the sun in the slightest. He stepped out onto the concrete and let it wash over him, his bronze skin absorbing the warmth.

He enjoyed the moment and then marched ahead. The dozens of guards surrounding him moved in perfect sync, keeping their lines tight.

The building ahead of the procession was like any other in the city. Normally, the Teacher would keep to the mountains, hiding out in his mansion for the sake of security. Out there, one could see an attack coming from miles away, even most aerial attacks save for the most potent ones the West was so fond of using on targets.

He grinned at the thought, the irony tickling his senses.

He'd just witnessed that kind of attack on his dummy targets the day before, hidden away in some secret headquarters in Liverpool.

The Teacher had done well, and he knew what awaited him inside the building as he approached the doors.

He climbed the steps and started to reach out to pull on a looped handle, but one of the guards beat him to it, bowed his head, and opened the door for him.

The Teacher gave a grateful nod and stepped across the threshold.

The building was a fortress. It was confined within a sparsely populated part of the city, occupied instead by mosques, shops, and factories, most of which were closed. Just to be safe, units had been positioned on key thoroughfares to ensure that no unauthorized eyes caught a glimpse of the convoy's precious cargo.

Inside the building, the temperature was easily fifteen degrees cooler than outside. The Teacher let the cool air envelop him and tingle his skin. He stood there for a moment with the door still open and guards filing in around him. On the exterior, the building looked like so many in the city, beige sun baked bricks with no sign of what was inside. Little shop signs or painted words and symbols typically identified most buildings. This one had none of that because what was inside wasn't for the public to see.

The heavy doors slammed shut behind the Teacher, and he gazed into the cavernous interior. The ceiling was thirty feet high, supported by massive stone pillars in three primary rows that ran the length of the structure. That length, too, was considerable. The building was at least two hundred yards from end to end.

Architecturally, the place was an Arabian warehouse. Nothing more. And that's exactly what the Teacher wanted.

Before him stood hundreds of his soldiers, all in neatly organized rows and columns. Each man wore the same black uniform with no identifying marks or clear affiliations. They held Kalashnikov rifles across their chests at an angle from waist to shoulder.

Behind them, along the walls of the building, were stacks upon stacks of wooden crates, metal bins, and shipping containers, all with different symbols, warnings, and labels applied to the sides to identify what was contained within.

The Teacher allowed a thin smile to crease his lips, and he nodded, raising his hands up to shoulder level, palms facing the ceiling. He paused for a long moment before saying anything, letting the drama build in the room until it was hanging like a dense fog.

"We have struck back," he said. His voice carried through the entire span of the building and echoed back.

A loud uproar burst from the rows of soldiers. They held their weapons into the air, screaming at the top of their lungs. The cacophony filled the room to an almost deafening level.

The Teacher kept his hands high in triumph, wearing the same satisfied grin. His eyes shifted over to a bald man to the right, in front of one of the columns. He was dressed like all the others, but there was no questioning he was some kind of officer in the Teacher's army.

The old man lowered his arms and walked toward his general. He stopped just in front of him and paused, then clapped his hand on a muscular shoulder.

"This is a great day, Aziz," the Teacher said. "We have landed a blow that will echo throughout history."

Aziz tried to keep a stoic expression, but pride leaked out of his dark eyes, gleaming in the dim light coming from single bulbs that hung from the ceiling.

The Teacher opened his arms and wrapped them around his trusted commander, embracing him tightly.

Aziz returned the embrace.

The noise in the room died down, and the old man stepped back to address the troops.

"This is only the beginning!" he shouted. "The infidels believed they were clever. They believed they were powerful. They believed that their evil plans could not be stopped!" He let the words hang in the room for a few seconds. "They were wrong!"

The crowd cheered again, once more raising their weapons high.

The Teacher let them enjoy the moment and waited until silence fell again.

"Now, the biggest thorn in our side is dead. The dragon that served the evil one is no more. Let this day be a warning to all who would challenge us; that we will not stand in the dark much longer, that our mighty Allah will deliver us from the sins of the wicked that have tainted this world. He will save us and will purge the earth through our hands."

Another uproar ensued, and the Teacher waved to the crowd for several seconds before he lowered his hand and motioned for Aziz to follow him. They walked away from the group as the lower-level officers started issuing orders to the troops.

The two men walked toward a makeshift office in the corner. It was nothing more than a frame of 2x4s with a plywood sheath.

"The men know what to do next, yes?" The Teacher asked the question even though he had almost no doubts as to what the answer would be.

"Yes, sir. They are ready and awaiting final instructions."

The old man nodded. His robes flitted around his body like a ghost in the wind. The hood around his face jiggled as he moved.

"Excellent."

They stepped into the little office, and Aziz closed the door. A modest round table sat in the center with matching chairs. An ornate metal teapot sat in the center of the table, paired with two porcelain teacups featuring symbols native to the land of Uzbekistan. Some were lines that formed squares like tiny mazes. Others were swirls and mosaic tiles of bright blue.

The smell of the hot tea filled the room and wafted into the Teacher's nostrils as he pulled up a chair and eased into it.

He didn't wait for his second-in-command to pour the drink, instead taking on the role of the servant and pouring a cup for them both as Aziz sat down across from him.

"Thank you, Teacher," he said with a nod and gratefully took the cup. He held it up, waiting for his boss to bless the drink.

The old man said a short prayer to Allah and then lifted the cup to his lips, taking a short sip. Then he placed the cup back on its saucer and leaned back.

After taking a drink himself, Aziz set his cup down and looked across at the Teacher. "Master, you know I would never question your decisions, your leadership."

"But you had concerns over my mission."

It was no secret. The doubt had been evident since the inception of the idea. Aziz had been against it from the start, but he also knew better than to go against the Teacher. Doing so would be treason, both to the cause and to Allah.

"I did. I wish you would have let me or one of the other men go."

The old man nodded. "It had to be me, Aziz. I had to see it for myself, dig into the underbelly of the snake so that I could rip its guts out with my own hands."

"You have done well, Master."

"Something like this has never been done before. It will go down in history as one of the greatest attacks ever carried out against the West."

The Teacher had carefully crafted the trap aimed directly at the agency responsible for so much chaos in the last few months. It had taken a good deal of time and crossing palms with silver to get the information he needed, but he finally learned who the Spanish woman was—at least by first name—and who she worked for.

Now she was dead, along with everyone in her little agency.

He didn't know the name of it, though he was certain it was a more secretive operation than the more well-known organizations: CIA, FBI, MI5, and the other subsidiaries of that ilk.

"It was a brave move, sir," Aziz said, lifting his cup and taking another sip.

He was correct in more ways than he could have imagined. The Teacher had gone through significant physical pain to make it look like he'd been tortured, at least a little. It would have to be real enough for the infidels to consider his testimony legitimate and his defection authentic.

Finding the agency was equally as trying a task, though after a series of fake "leaks", eventually someone came calling. All one had to do was put the information out there for the right people to find, and sooner or later, the fish would take the bait.

As far as he'd known, no warriors of his kind had ever attempted anything like it before, going into a highly secure government agency to destroy it from within. He'd heard of it in the history books, reading about the world wars and the spy intrigue that ensued as well as followed throughout the Cold War.

Even then, as cunning as his plan was, a typical move for someone in his position would have been to assign the mission to a soldier underneath him. Indeed, Aziz had offered—no, begged—to be the one to go. He feared for the Teacher's life and worried that, if caught, their movement would stall and the men would lose hope as well as faith.

Most terrorist organizations operated in such a manner. The leaders were never the ones strapping bombs to their chests and walking into a marketplace. They were pulling the strings from a secure cave deep in the mountains somewhere.

Fortune, the Teacher believed, favored the bold.

Now he was the unquestioned leader to not only these men but also thousands more that would rally to their cause. Once the word spread that the Teacher had infiltrated a highly secure Western agency and brought it to its knees, recruits would flood in by the hundreds every day. Their fledgling operation would grow exponentially, spurred on by the daring actions of this man sitting across from Aziz.

"I assume the preparations are in place for the next phase of our operation?" The Teacher raised his cup again, as well as a bushy eyebrow.

"Yes, sir. Everything you have ordered is being carried out as we speak. The next phase will be ready to initiate in thirty-six hours."

The Teacher pursed his lips, showing he was impressed. Despite implicitly trusting his second-in-command, things could always be slowed down when initiating a large-scale operation such as this. Several hundred people were involved. Logistics were a nightmare due to the scope of the project. Somehow, though, Aziz had managed to pull it off.

"Excellent. Prepare the men to attack the first targets in two days. We will hit them hard and fast, all at once."

"Yes, sir." Aziz didn't need to be reminded of how the operation was going to go. He'd set up the whole thing, but he also never corrected the Teacher. He knew better.

"Soon, my friend, we will bring the world to its knees. And when we do, the great cleansing can finally take place."

7

LYON, FRANCE

Adriana had been uncomfortable from the moment she walked into the huge room. It wasn't the computer screens, the dozens of people scurrying around with tablets in their hand or files under their arm. It also wasn't the people in the suits with high-ranking, top secret clearance—if that's what it was called. The cause of her discomfort was the overwhelming feeling that she didn't belong in a room full of international police.

She'd heard of Interpol many times throughout her life. Most of those instances were while watching movies. To her knowledge, she'd never had any direct interactions with any of their officers, though it was probable she had and simply didn't know it.

Her eyes flashed to a screen on a desk ten feet away. A picture of a man with long brown hair and an olive complexion staring straight ahead with cold, vapid eyes filled the left side of the monitor. The other half was a picture of his back that displayed a huge owl tattoo. The artwork covered almost his entire back all the way up to his shoulders. Apparently, the man was one of the most wanted international murderers on their list.

The Teacher, she supposed, would be moving up on those charts quickly.

Interpol had offices throughout the world, but their main headquarters was in Lyon, France. It was a city Adriana had visited several times. She preferred it to Paris in many ways, one of which was the smaller size. All of the culture, less of the hustle and bustle. At least that's how she viewed it.

With many of her resources destroyed in the explosion, June knew they had to leverage someone else's. She had connections with MI5 in London, and truth be told, that would have been more convenient in many ways, but June also knew that some of the other agencies under direct government control were less than cooperative with her outfit. She'd run into conflicts on numerous occasions when trying to get information from the CIA, FBI, MI5, and others.

Maybe they were jealous. Or perhaps they simply didn't trust an agency that operated out of the parameters to which they adhered. It could have been a little of both.

June didn't care. It had never really been an issue before. She had everything she needed in-house. Except now her house was a pile of smoldering rubble near the River Mersey.

Adriana watched as her friend chatted with a man in a navy-blue blazer, black tie, and matching blue pants. His hair was cropped short in a military style, showing off his high forehead. A sharply sloping nose protruded from his face between two keen brown eyes. His wide jaw gave the impression of authority that matched the intensity of his gaze that never seemed to waver. She wondered if he wore that same look while he was eating dinner with his kids or if the guy ever softened.

Their heads bobbed up and down as the two exchanged information and questions. Adriana and June had only been there for an hour, waiting fifteen minutes before being shown into the war room, or whatever it was called. That's what Adriana called it. They were, after all, going to war against crime across the entire planet.

June gave a final nod and then motioned toward Adriana. The Spaniard perked up, straightening her back and stiffening her shoulders as the two made their way over to where she stood. June raised a hand as if displaying a rare vase in a private gallery.

"This is Adriana Villa," June said when they stopped a few feet away. "One of my best assets."

The description sounded cold, unaffectionate, but Adriana understood why. She couldn't very well introduce her as a personal friend. Things had to remain extremely professional, especially in this environment.

The man gave a courteous nod and extended his hand, shaking Adriana's with a grip she found surprisingly infirm.

"A pleasure to meet you," he said. "My name is Olivier Pavard, at your service." His thick French accent came as no surprise.

"Likewise." She let go of his hand and offered a polite smile.

"That name, it is Spanish, no?"

"Oui," she confirmed in his native language. The response elicited a similar grin.

"June told me everything. Of course, we knew about the attacks a few minutes after they happened. This man, the Teacher, wasn't on our radar before. We knew about his organization, the Red Ring, and that there was a leader running their operation."

"But you didn't know who he was or what he looked like."

His head drooped a few millimeters. "Precisely. He was a ghost, a total mystery." Pavard motioned for the two women to follow, and he turned away, starting down the aisle between workstations. He pointed to a big screen in the front of the room. "We track some of the most wanted criminals in the world, from vicious murderers and terrorists to cyber criminals. Unfortunately, the latter often proves extremely difficult to track."

"Cyber criminals?" Adriana asked. She knew what they were but was surprised at his comment. "I would think they might be easier to find since they leave a trail."

"That's the problem," Pavard said, glancing over his shoulder at her. "They know how to cover their tracks. Many of them are geniuses, which means they are extremely careful and know what we're looking for. It's difficult to stay a step ahead of people like that."

"Because they're always a step ahead."

"Oui."

Pavard turned right at the end of the aisle. He walked in long strides and being a few inches over six feet, the two women had to double their pace to keep up. He made his way down the path between desks to a set of doors at the end and pushed through them. Once they were in the next hall, away from the noise of the previous room, he slowed his pace.

"Shame about the people you lost," he said in a somber tone. "I know it would be devastating if something like that happened here. My condolences."

"I appreciate that," June said.

"I have to be honest. I'm a little surprised you came to me, but I will do everything I can to help. We'll set you up with offices and any personnel you might need."

"That won't be necessary, Olivier."

He glanced over his shoulder at her with eyebrows arched. "Non?"

"Non, to the people," she clarified. "Resources, though, we could use."

"Name it."

He whirled to the left and motioned them into a corner office that looked out onto a forested area just across from the parking lot. The city of Lyon loomed just beyond in the distance.

Olivier stepped behind his desk and eased into his seat, folding one leg over a knee and steepling his fingers in front of his chest. The two women found chairs across from him and made themselves comfortable.

"I need any camera footage you can scrounge up from the two attack sites. I want to know who the two men were that took our informant."

"Done."

That was easy, Adriana thought.

"I also need to check the footage from every major airport within a six-hour drive of Liverpool. Even Charles de Gaulle if you can manage it."

He tapped the tips of his fingers together, considering the request. "That's a big one, non?"

"Oui," June agreed. "I know. And I also realize that is a huge tax on your people. But Olivier, if we don't find this guy, I'm concerned the next thing he's going to do will be far worse than Liverpool."

The concern on the Frenchman's face was etched in the lines across his forehead. "Yes, I was afraid you were going to say that."

"We've been tracking this group for a while now," Adriana finally spoke up. "They are planning something big; that much we know."

"Adriana helped us cripple their operations. We destroyed millions of dollars' worth of weapons and tech, but apparently, that was only the tip of the iceberg."

"I hadn't heard about that," Pavard confessed.

That wasn't a surprise to either woman. That was, after all, the purpose of Shadow Cell, to operate in total secrecy, beyond that which most government funded groups could achieve. Bureaucracy slowed things down, adhered to agendas and laws. June's organization could operate outside those boundaries, and while some might suggest they were cowboys trying to police the world, sometimes cowboys were what was needed. Especially when it came to situations like the one they were facing.

"We kept it quiet," June offered.

Pavard bit his bottom lip and nodded, understanding. He had his own set of rules he had to play by, but now and then he'd bend them almost to the point of breaking. He understood that sometimes one had to get dirty to get rid of the crap in society. More times than not, he wished he could do what these two women were doing, getting into the thick of it, taking the fight to the bad guys without any constraints except their own conscience.

"I'll do whatever I can, but what you're asking…it could take some time."

"I know. And that's not a luxury we have."

"When do you think they're going to make their next move?"

June shook her head. "It's anyone's guess, but I would say soon."

"Possible targets?"

"Could be anything. I know that security is already tight all over Europe for concerts and soccer...football games." She corrected herself to use the regional term. "Sorry, American."

He chuckled and waved a dismissive hand.

"Yes," he agreed, "and in light of the Liverpool incident, security will be more heightened all over the continent for those matches and any concerts that are scheduled for the upcoming season."

That was what happened whenever something like this occurred. Then, as time wore on, security would become laxer until another tragedy. It was human nature. June and Adriana both knew that, as did Pavard.

"Any other potentials?" he asked.

The two women drew in long breaths and exhaled at the same time, the universal signal for "I don't know."

"I would say that the usual targets would be in play, but the last several years, terrorist attacks have come in unusual places and hitting common locations that are nearly impossible to protect without instigating some kind of martial-law scenario."

"Curfews?"

"You know as well as I do how difficult those can be to enforce and uphold. Not to mention the fact that the people would revolt against something like that were you to try to put it into place across the entire continent."

"Indeed. What then?"

"Proceed as normal. It's the only thing we can do without massive upheaval."

"And wait for another attack?"

"We won't be waiting," Adriana cut in. "Find us this Teacher and the men who got him out of our custody. Do that, and we'll make sure nothing bad happens."

She stared into his eyes and out the back of his skull.

There was no mistaking the resolve in her gaze. "You were there, hmm? In Liverpool?"

"I was in the car with the old man."

His eyes widened at the confession. "It's a miracle you're alive."

"Sí." She used her native tongue.

"Good. Well, I will put my best people on it right away. And I will personally oversee things until we can track down this villain and bring him to justice."

"Thank you, Olivier," June said with a nod. "I appreciate it."

A knock at the door interrupted their conversation. Pavard looked up and saw a tall, dark-skinned woman in a burgundy business suit. He waved her in. She poked her head through a narrow gap. "They need you on the fourth floor, sir." Her accent was English. Based on that and her appearance, Adriana and June figured she was of Indian descent.

"Okay, tell them I'll be right there."

Pavard pushed himself out of his chair with both hands. "Please excuse me. Make yourselves at home, and don't hesitate to ask for anything."

"Thank you," the women said together.

He walked to the door and followed the woman out, disappearing around the corner toward the elevators.

Adriana turned to her friend. "What in the world did you do for him that put him so deep in your debt?"

June noticed the raised eyebrow on Adriana's forehead and quickly shook off the insinuation. "Nothing scandalous, I promise you that."

"You sure? Because he seems like he would do pretty much anything for you."

"One of the tricks of this trade is to always put yourself into a position of power, or at least where you can use leverage."

The befuddled look on Adriana's face told June to elaborate.

"Olivier was looking for someone a few years ago, a guy who'd been abducting young girls and then killing them."

"A serial killer."

"Of sorts, yes. Olivier was a detective at the time. He didn't have any leads to go on. The killer was extremely clever when it came to hiding his tracks."

"Not clever enough."

"He almost was. It took one slip for me to find him. When I did, I knew that I could take him in myself, execute him, and dump his worthless body in a river—or I could do something else."

"You played the long game," Adriana realized out loud.

"Exactly. I didn't need credit, and I certainly wasn't seeking any kind of advancement, but I knew that someday, if I put that killer into Olivier's hands, he could be in a position to help me. He was already a rising star. I just had to light the fire."

June was resourceful; Adriana had to give her that.

"Let's just hope he can help us."

"He will," June insisted. "If any of those three men show their faces in Europe, Olivier can find them."

8

MALMO, SWEDEN

The crowd roared as the two teams sprinted down the field toward the goal on the west end. Most of the contingent in the stands donned the yellow and blue of the Swedish flag, while a small pocket in the corner proudly displayed white and blue, the colors of Finland.

The two nations were embroiled in a tight clash to see who would advance to the World Cup the following summer. It had been a close race, but only one of them would move on. The other would have four years to think about what they'd done wrong and try to fix it.

Johan Korgsen yelled at the top of his lungs right up to the point when Sweden fired a shot over the right corner of the goal, only missing by inches. The entire crowd made the same disappointed sound, only to get roaring again as the ball was put back in play by the Finnish goalkeeper.

Johan had never been to an international football game before. He'd seen his favorite club, Malmö, play on several occasions. His parents tried to take him to at least three games a year. Seeing the Swedish international team, though, was a special treat and one he would never forget.

The game was deadlocked at 1-1 as they neared the halftime

break, but Johan just knew that more goals were coming in the second half. There was just this feeling on the pitch that both teams were playing with a desperate intensity, and that sense permeated the crowd by the tens of thousands.

Johan stared with rapt wonder as one of his favorite players surged forward through the center of the field, dipping the ball out wide to one of the wings. An attacking midfielder sprinted ahead, chasing down the ball in midstride and taking a quick touch with the top of his foot. A tap, a dip of the head, then another tap, and he was by the defender, again charging down the touch-line toward the corner flag.

The winger picked his head up for a moment, noting the position of his center forward.

Johan wished he was playing a video game at that very moment, so he could take control of the players and send the perfect pass through or over the top to his striker. Alas, he was without any control and had to keep watching and hoping.

Luckily, the midfielder read Johan's mind. At least that's what the boy wanted to believe. The man with the ball took a huge step, planted his left foot, and swung his right leg. The right foot struck the ball with incredible energy and sent it looping across the field into the eighteen-yard box. The forward pumped his legs harder, seeing the moment flash before his eyes. He knew this was it, a chance to take the lead in an all-important moment just before halftime.

The striker leaped into the air just inside the eighteen-yard line and caught the ball with his chest, dropping it to the right foot in a deft move of grace and control. The defender behind him grappled at his shoulder, his shirt, anything he could find to slow the forward down, but he stumbled and fell forward.

Sensing his moment, the forward tilted his head up as he charged ahead, catching a glimpse of the goalkeeper as he rushed forward to cut down the angle.

The center forward knew that was coming and took a quick touch to the right. It shortened his angle of attack but opened a window on the goalkeeper's left side that wouldn't have been there otherwise.

The keeper lunged to his left as the forward swung his foot through the ball, striking it with incredible force. The goalkeeper's hands shot out to one side, his right leg bending awkwardly in an attempt to cover every possible opening.

The ball sailed over the goalkeeper's hands and flew rapidly toward the goal. It was too far away to see from where he sat, but Johan thought for certain he'd seen the striker crack a smile.

Then, as suddenly as crowd reached the brink of eruption, the moment was lost as the ball bounced off the crossbar, glancing over the top of the net and into the crowd beyond.

The referee blew his whistle among tens of thousands of groans.

Johan exhaled and slumped into his seat. He wasn't worried. They still had the second half to get ahead, and he felt confident that's exactly what was going to happen.

"That was a great first half, huh, Son?"

Johan turned to his father and grinned, nodding. "It sure was. I thought we were going to take the lead on that last shot."

"Well, there's plenty of time left. Maybe we can get another one or even two before the game is over."

"I hope so."

"Either way, it's been a fun game so far."

Johan beamed. "Yes, it has. Thank you so much for bringing me. This is so exciting."

His father reached out an arm and put it around Johan's shoulders, clapping him on the arm. "I'm glad you're having a good time." Then his dad turned and looked up the stairs to the exit leading out onto the mezzanine. "Would you like a snack or something else to drink?"

"Sure."

"It's a bit warmer than usual, isn't it?"

Johan nodded, and then he saw something floating toward them. A miniature white blimp, around eight feet long, three feet wide, and three feet tall, driven with twin propeller fans in the front and back, was cruising over the crowd. He noticed another one on the other side of the stadium. Each blimp was equipped with a pair of white tubes extending out from the bottom.

"What's that?" Johan asked.

His father turned toward the little dirigible and laughed. "Looks like a little halftime entertainment."

Suddenly, a fine mist started spraying out tiny holes in the white metal tube under the blimp, raining cool moisture down on the crowd.

People raised their hands and stood up, letting the man-made precipitation sprinkle over them, cooling their skin against the heat.

"Oh, it's a mister," Johan's father realized. "I've seen these before."

"Me, too," Johan added quickly. "They have them at some of the amusement parks in the summer to cool people off, though I've never seen one on a blimp like that before. That's so neat."

The boy watched with wonder in his eyes as the lumbering aircraft coasted slowly over the crowd, drifting toward him. More than a few drunken fans tilted their heads back and opened their mouths, letting the mist waft onto their thirsty tongues. Johan put up his hands and tilted his head back, ready to feel the relieving moisture on his skin.

The blimp turned right, though, and drifted upward toward the second level of the stadium, continuing to spray the fans below as they cheered and waved at the blimp, as if its driver was on board the thing.

"Aw," Johan said with a disappointed moan. "I wanted it to spray us. I bet that mist feels really good."

"Maybe it will come around this way again," his father said. "Or that other one might fly over us." He pointed at the other blimp making its way around the opposite side of the stadium.

Johan's father could see the disappointment in the boy's eyes. It was a silly thing, he knew, but he also remembered what it was like to be young. Sometimes, silly things were what mattered most to kids.

"Come on, Son. Let's go get something to drink. Perhaps by the time we get back to our seats the blimp will be returning to this section."

The boy nodded eagerly, satisfied with his dad's solution.

The two made their way out of their row and up the steps, disappearing through the tunnel and out onto the mezzanine while the crowd below continued their frenzied revelry over the novel flying machines.

9

LYON

June stood in the back of the room with her arms crossed. She preferred standing for meetings like this as opposed to being cramped in a big leather back chair at the end of the table.

Adriana was by her side, listening with focused intensity to the presentation.

The screen at the other end of the boardroom showed a man with black hair and eyebrows. It was a photo taken by one of the street cameras in Liverpool, just before the attacks began.

Adriana recognized the guy immediately.

"We don't have a positive ID on these two yet," the young Interpol detective said. He clicked a button on the remote in his hand, and the screen changed to the other guy from the Liverpool attack. It was from a similar angle, taken in black and white by a traffic camera.

The presenter clicked the button again, and they were given a new view of the men, this time together, surrounded by hundreds of other people.

"Are those loading docks?" Adriana asked.

"Yes. Pavard requested that we also scan images from any ports of entry within the same perimeter you requested for the airport surveillance footage."

Adriana's eyebrows flicked up for a second in surprise. These guys *were* thorough.

The team Pavard assigned to help June and Adriana had worked around the clock for the last twenty-four hours, only taking a few hours to catch some sleep in shifts. There were eight people in the room, and every single one of them needed a shower and a good night's rest. If they hadn't been tracking down a dangerous terrorist, June might have felt bad for the investigators, but finding this man and his henchmen as soon as possible was paramount above all else, even personal well-being and hygiene.

She had to give them credit. They were relentless. Pavard had chosen some of his best—or at least that was the impression June was getting.

"They took a boat across the channel to Dunkirk," the detective continued. "From there, they made their way across the border into Belgium." He flashed another picture on the screen of the men dressed in different clothes, passing through the border between France and Belgium. "We lost them shortly after that."

June sighed, frustrated. "So, that means they could be anywhere."

"We're checking the footage from the regional and international airports in Belgium. Antwerp, Bruges, Brussels, but it will take some time. We have alerted the authorities in those cities to be on the lookout for these three, but even with their help it could be another day or two before we have anything."

"By then, they could be back in whatever cave they crawled out of," June said with derision.

"Indeed. We're doing the best we can, but these men had a plan in place and executed it with extreme precision."

June ran her fingers through the hair on the left side. A rogue strand dangled from her usually perfectly tight ponytail. She considered the intel she'd been given and ran through several options in her mind. None of them were great, and more questions than had been answered surfaced in the muck.

"We need to know where these guys came from," Adriana said,

cutting into the silence. "Is it possible to cross-reference those images with airports around the world?"

The guy at the head of the table pursed his lips and nodded, glancing at some of the other team members to confirm. They nodded as well.

A woman with dark red hair in a gray jacket and matching skirt was sitting next to him. She turned to Adriana. "Yes, we've had facial recognition software for several years now. Although now it is much more advanced, obviously. We could run checks across the entire planet, though that would take time."

Adriana shook her head. "That won't be necessary."

"No?" The woman's French accent was deep.

"Isolate it to the Middle East. From Syria to Pakistan, all the way north to Kazakhstan and everywhere in between. Include Albania in that search, too."

"Albania?"

"We recently found some of the Red Ring's operations going on in Albania," June explained. "Those locations were significantly disabled, but it's possible these guys might have gone there. I agree with Adriana. Check there just to be sure."

"Certainly," the man by the screen said.

People were taking furious notes on paper or on their tablets, getting every detail to make sure they didn't miss a thing.

"The second you find out who any of these guys are or where they came from, you let me know." June's voice was commanding, decisive. There was no doubt in the room who was running the show, and not a soul questioned her leadership. "You've all seen what happened in Liverpool. We can't let that happen again. Understood?"

Everyone in the room nodded.

"Okay, let's find these guys and take them down."

One by one, the team of investigators filed out of the room, leaving Adriana and June alone.

June walked over to the door and closed it, slumping down into the closest chair. She gazed out the window at the city of Lyon with its ancient cathedral spires, colorful old buildings, and a few skyscrapers off in the distance. Somewhere in the sprawling city, the river wound through the structures, the lifeblood of the aged town. On a hilltop, a massive fortress stood against the backdrop of a clear azure sky.

She wanted to appreciate the view, even get out and enjoy the city for a few hours, take in the culture, and maybe get a bite from one of the fabled French restaurants in town.

That couldn't happen.

She absently rubbed her eyes and yawned.

"You need some sleep," Adriana observed, making her way to the other side of the table and finding a seat of her own.

June gave the faintest shake of her head. "No time for that. We could get word of those terrorists' whereabouts at any moment. When we do, I want to be ready to go."

"I know, but you also need to rest. You won't be any good in a fight if it comes to that and you're exhausted."

"I'll be fine, but thanks for your concern. I do appreciate it."

Adriana shrugged. "I understand. You and I aren't that different."

June snorted a laugh, showing she agreed. "Thanks for thinking of the facial recognition software. My mind is in a million places. I can't believe I didn't think of that."

"They were likely already running cross-checks on that anyway. A little focus never hurts, though."

"True. So, you think they went back to the Middle East?"

"Yes. You don't?"

June rolled her shoulders and tossed her head from one side to the other, indicating she wasn't sure. "I mean, that would be the obvious thing, right? But is it too obvious?"

"You're more of an expert on this kind of stuff than me," Adriana confessed. "My main aim at checking those airports wasn't to find out where they went, though, but where they came from. If we can figure out where those men flew in from, we might be able to track them down to their origin. Do that, and we can find where the rats are hiding."

"Sounds like a long shot."

"And a time-consuming one at that. Let's just hope that the group your friend Pavard gave us can work fast. The sooner we locate those goons, the sooner we can track down the Teacher."

June noticed the remote control sitting nearby and scooped it up. She pressed the power button, turning on the television hanging from the wall at the far end of the room.

"What are you doing?" Adriana asked.

"Checking the news. I want to see if there are any updates on Liverpool."

"You trust the media?"

June fired a sidelong glance at her friend that said it all. "You know better than that, but at least we can see if there are any new developments."

She flipped through the channels until she found a blonde woman in a red suit sitting behind a news desk. She was speaking in French, which was fine for June and Adriana since they both spoke it fluently. The headline in the top right corner read "Flu Outbreak in Sweden."

"Reports are coming in of a widespread influenza outbreak in Sweden and Finland. This strain of the virus seems to work faster than others and has already put hundreds of people in critical condition with tens of thousands more showing early symptoms of the illness. Medical teams are working to figure out the point of origin for this virus, but as yet have no answers. Due to the fact that the outbreak has affected citizens of Finland and Sweden combined, some experts have suggested that the virus originated at the recent football match between the two nations that took place in Malmö yesterday."

Adriana frowned. "Yesterday?"

June turned to her friend with a curious expression on her face. "What about it?"

"Viruses don't work that fast. Flu especially. It has a forty-eight-hour gestation period before it kicks in."

"I'm not medically trained. Could you explain that to me in English?"

"It means that if you catch the flu, you won't start showing symptoms for two days."

"Ah. So...?"

"So, this is some kind of super virus. If what that news anchor is saying is correct, it would have kicked in in less than twenty-four hours."

June scrunched her face, trying to understand what all this meant. "Which would make this some kind of super virus?"

"Exactly," Adriana nodded.

"Wow. That's heavy."

The topic struck close to home for Adriana. She remembered her grandparents talking about the Spanish flu pandemic that killed between fifty and a hundred million people worldwide. They'd been small children when it happened, but their parents talked of it often. Friends and loved ones had died. Many of their friends lost children who'd previously been healthy. It turned out to be one of the deadliest natural disasters in the course of human history, though conspiracy theorists had their own ideas about how it had happened.

Adriana recalled seeing a television show where a biologist suggested that the outbreak was a deliberate attack on humanity. Who had been responsible for the attack, the biologist didn't know, but he was certain that the disease had been engineered to take down a wide swath of the population.

If that was the case, the engineer of death had been successful. People on remote islands caught the virus. Even those in the far reaches of the Arctic weren't immune to it.

Seeing this news report brought all those stories back to Adriana's mind.

"A football match," she muttered absently.

"What?" June looked at the screen and then back at her friend.

"That anchor said that authorities believe this virus spread from the football match between Sweden and Finland."

"So?"

Adriana's mind raced as she connected dots that had no business being drawn together. "What...what if this was an attack?"

"An attack? The flu?" June glanced back to the screen.

"Terrorists have been working on stuff like this for years. Bioweapons can take on many forms, right?"

"Sure."

"Anthrax, chemical weapons, they'll use anything they can."

"Where are you going with all this?"

Adriana leaned forward and pointed over her shoulder at the television. "The attack in Liverpool. Now a few days later this happens? Is it a coincidence?"

Now she had June's attention. "You're saying that the Red Ring created a superbug and somehow snuck it into a soccer game?"

Adriana didn't try to correct her on the terminology of the sport. It wasn't the time or place. "It's possible."

June frowned. "It sounds like a stretch to me. You sure you're not reaching?"

"Maybe I am. Maybe it is a stretch, but think about it."

"I *am* thinking about it. Adriana, people get sick. Sometimes, lots of people get sick. That's how these things spread. One person contracts something, sneezes into a crowd, and thirty more of them catch it. That's the way it works."

Adriana considered her friend's point. Perhaps she *was* reaching, looking for answers where there were none. Still, something deep down in her gut told her this was more than a coincidence.

"The ruse the old man played with us," she blurted the words and then realized they didn't make sense. "He played us, right?"

"Seems that way."

"He did. He made us think we were taking out high-priority targets that would weaken the Red Ring."

"Yeah, so?"

"It's a shell game. He made us think we were taking out bombs, guns, ammunition. The whole time, his plan wasn't brute-force attacks with those kinds of weapons. It was subtler, deadlier. Armed forces and anti-terrorist units can fight battles against guns and bombs. The rules of engagement become clear in those scenarios, and there is no way that the terrorists can win in the end."

"What are you saying?" June arched one eyebrow.

"I'm saying that this Teacher person isn't stupid. He knows he can't win a direct battle with the militaries of the world."

"That's why they hijack planes, bomb churches or mosques, use suicide bombers."

"All those tactics are to make statements, to cause trouble, and to change the way of life in the free world. They're political and religious moves. But germ warfare, that's a war they can win. If they have the right recipe for a superbug, it could cause hundreds of millions of deaths. Maybe billions if put in the right place."

"Like the Spanish epidemic."

"Nearly 5 percent of the world's population died from that."

June made a tiny hole with her lips and blew air through it, letting out a faint whistle. "That was back when travel was pretty much limited to boats and trains."

"The world is connected now," Adriana continued her point. "If something like that happened today, it could be far worse."

"To be fair, we're better equipped to handle medical crises like that."

"Are we? When that anthrax scare happened several years ago, there weren't enough antibiotics to go around. Not to mention the fact that doctors have been prescribing those so much over the years, humans are building up a resistance to them."

"Resistance?"

"I have friends in the medical profession that are concerned our antibiotics won't be as effective against something like this, if at all."

"Okay," June relented. "What do you want to do about it? People are already sick. If your theory is correct, it might already be too late."

"Maybe. Maybe not. The Teacher is smart, smarter than we initially gave him credit for. This is a venture of sorts. Any good venture starts with a soft launch."

"You're saying this was a test run?"

Adriana nodded. "I think it might be."

"All right then. What's the plan?"

"You stay here and work on finding those men who took the Teacher."

"And you?"

Adriana stood up and stared at the television. "I'm going to Malmö."

"Um, are you sure that's a good idea? I don't want you getting sick with whatever this flu is."

"I'll be fine," Adriana said. She tried to sound confident, but the stories her grandparents had shared echoed in her mind, horrible visions of people in beds, rows and rows of them, filling barren rooms with the sick and dying. She stiffened her resolve. "I have to get to the bottom of this. If I can figure out how they delivered this bug—"

"If they did it," June interrupted.

"Yes, if this is a deliberate attack, I need to find out how they did it so we can keep it from happening elsewhere."

June's face looked uneasy. She didn't like the idea of her friend going into a place where there was an outbreak of some strange illness. She also knew once Adriana's mind was made up, there was no changing it.

"Okay," she said. "Be careful."

"You know me better than that."

"Yeah. I know. You're never careful."

10

UZBEKISTAN

The Teacher sat in a lavish living room, sipping on a cup of hot tea as he watched the news reports roll in on the flatscreen. Thousands of people were on the verge of death in Sweden and Finland, their bodies ravaged by a more aggressive form of influenza than the world had seen in a hundred years.

He grinned as he saw the images of sinners suffering at the hands of a microorganism. Women and children were crying in hospitals and on the streets. Some were holding prayer vigils outside the churches in Stockholm and Malmö. Then there was footage of people in biohazard outfits working on isolating the source of the disease.

The experts had pinpointed ground zero of the outbreak, but they still had no idea how it happened. The Teacher grinned. They would likely never put two and two together. The delivery method had been right in front of their eyes, for forty thousand people to see, and yet they were too wrapped up in their foolish entertainment to notice.

He'd seen footage from the blimp cameras of drunken idiots standing under the mist as it poured down from above. Some of them even opened their mouths, letting the virus sprinkle directly onto their tongues. Those people were likely the first to show early symptoms, and the Teacher knew they would also be among the first to die.

He took another sip of tea and set the cup on a saucer on the table in front of him. Then he leaned back and stretched out his arms, letting the cool air from a ceiling fan wash over him.

Aziz walked into the room from a doorway to the left and stopped short of the couch, waiting to be addressed by his leader.

"Ah, my old friend. Come, sit. I was just enjoying the fruits of our labors."

Aziz did as told and helped himself to a seat in a leather chair next to the sofa. He looked up at the screen with grim pride. "How many dead, sir?"

"None yet, but that's only a matter of time. This virus works much faster than most other strains of the flu. Our biologists did well."

"Indeed."

"It appears that our test run has been a tremendous success, Aziz. That means we can go ahead with phase two of the plan."

"Yes, sir."

The Teacher had been planning this for years. It took an incredible amount of time even to find the right people for the job. Recruiting biologists with the intelligence and experience required to genetically engineer a superbug had proved difficult, to say the least. Finding *any* new recruits was a difficult matter. The utmost caution had to be exercised to keep off the radar of governments and their agencies who were hunting down terrorists. Of course, the Teacher despised that term, *terrorists*. It made them sound like the villains.

He knew it was a tool of the Western media, a way to make men like him look like the bad guys. Doing so gave the West a sense of righteousness, of heroic purpose. That couldn't have been further from the truth. The Teacher wasn't out to just murder millions of people. It was a cleansing, something the scriptures foretold. He was simply ushering it forward. Sometimes, people had to die to pave the way for a better world, a world that would worship the one true god and follow in his path. And of course, at the forefront of that battle and the subsequent new world would be the Teacher, leading them to glory.

"You want us to begin putting the next pieces in place, sir?" Aziz asked. He was staring at the screen and then turned his head toward the Teacher after he spoke.

"Yes. Deliver the virus to all of the target cities, but do it one at a time."

"One at a time?" He wasn't questioning the Teacher's decision rather the change of strategy.

They'd discussed the plan more times than Aziz could count. The virus would be distributed across the major continents, striking major cities along the coasts. It was to be done all at once, though, not piecemeal. The idea was to strike with a biological blitzkrieg, hitting massive population centers all in one broad stroke. The world's medical response teams and emergency crisis intervention units would be unable to handle the sudden and overwhelming pandemic. What the Teacher was saying now represented a huge change in the plan.

"I'm not questioning your judgment," Aziz was quick to correct. "I would never."

"But we discussed another plan. I know." The Teacher's voice was calming, his expression matching it. "But there is another thing to consider, my old friend. Now that we have struck this mighty blow, the infidels will be on watch for it."

"You think they know?"

"Doubtful. However, it's only a matter of time. To be safe, I think it prudent to slip our virus into the major ports one at a time, leaking it into cities here and there to make it look more natural."

Aziz immediately understood the logic. "If we were to attack a dozen cities at once, they would know for certain it was deliberate."

"Precisely."

Such a move would put everyone on alert. Every military, government agency, and security team on the planet would be looking for them or anything remotely suspicious.

"What's the next target, sir?"

The Teacher flashed a devilish grin. "We will make it look as natural as possible, my friend. This first round will, no doubt, spread through Denmark and Norway, taking a natural course. Perhaps we should help it along. Saint Petersburg in Russia is one. Then we hit Amsterdam after that."

Aziz pulled out his phone and opened a map on the screen. He looked at the two cities. "An excellent plan, sir. It will look like the virus is spreading naturally in both directions from the epicenter."

"Yes. Once we have hit those two targets, it will continue to spread like a raging fire in a dry forest. No one will be able to stop it. Once that happens, we will hit Asia. And then North and South America."

"The world will be brought to its knees."

"Indeed. And this will make any other natural disaster in history look insignificant."

He took a sip of his tea and held the cup, staring into the television screen as the news reports continued to come through.

"How many do you think will die, Teacher?"

"Difficult to say. Our scientists say it could be hundreds of millions, but the highest projections suggest a full 15 percent of the population could perish."

Aziz raised both eyebrows. "That many?"

The Teacher nodded. "Yes. Perhaps even more. Once the nations of the world are crippled and their governments and economies crumble, our armies will begin the process of exterminating the infidels once and for all."

11

MALMO

Adriana stepped out of the cab and onto the sidewalk in front of the Skåne University Hospital. Reporters crowded the sidewalk and spilled over the curb and onto the street, their camera crews running nonstop to catch any breaking footage that came out of the building.

Police stood at all the entrances, keeping out the news crews to protect the families and the patients within who were being treated for the sudden and vicious flu outbreak. An ambulance rumbled by, swinging into a roundabout in front of the emergency room entrance. When the vehicle came to a stop, the back doors swung open, and EMTs climbed out with masks covering their faces and blue latex gloves on their hands. They lowered a gurney out onto the pavement. The latest victim of the outbreak was an elderly woman. Her red eyes streamed tears down both sides of her face, unable to keep the ducts from leaking. The woman had an oxygen mask over her mouth and nose.

Adriana shook her head and sighed.

She needed to get into the hospital, but the cops at the door were only letting in patients and next of kin. She watched as the EMTs rolled the elderly woman toward the doors. The solution hit her immediately.

Adriana rushed ahead, chasing after the gurney, careful to stay a few long strides behind.

When they reached the door, the cops stepped aside to let the emergency workers through. One of them put out a hand toward Adriana.

"Sorry, family and patients only."

"That's my grandmother," Adriana lied. "I need to stay with her. She has this flu."

Adriana did her best to hide her Spanish accent, which ended up causing it to sound a little more Swedish than she might have hoped.

The cop looked her up and down and then motioned her through the sliding doors. The second she was through, the two men in uniform stepped back in front of the portal, blocking it for anyone else.

Inside, the building looked eerily similar to the hospital Adriana had left in Liverpool just a few days before. There were subtle differences: the architecture, the layout, and the fact that the halls weren't lined with bleeding people from an explosion or with skin blackened from smoke and debris.

She kept up with the elderly woman for ten seconds and then veered off to the right, down a hallway leading to a waiting room.

Adriana had had a few hours on her flight to Copenhagen to figure out some sort of play, but the truth was she was still in the dark as to what she needed to do to even begin this investigation.

The big problem in the back of her mind was that if she was correct about the Red Ring being behind this influenza outbreak, then she was already on borrowed time and there was sure to be another attack of this kind in the near future. Whatever the timeline was, she didn't know it, and that meant she had to make every second count.

She stopped near a series of elevators and looked around. Her eyes were wide with the deer-in-the-headlights look. For the first time in a while, she was out of her element. This was an investigation. She didn't know the first thing about conducting an investigation.

Or did she?

Adriana had spent the better part of the last decade tracking down stolen art from World War II and returning it to families or governments in Europe. She snapped her head to shake off the doubts. She could do this. She'd figured out ancient riddles in long-dead languages and tracked artifacts that no one believed still existed.

She could find the source of this scourge.

A sign to her left indicated there was a waiting room down the hall. Waiting rooms had people. People were witnesses. It wasn't much, but it was as good a place to start as any. She knew the cops weren't going to talk to her. The doctors and nurses were too busy treating patients by the hundreds.

Her mind made up, Adriana strode down the hall and around the corner to the right where another placard pointed toward the waiting room. She kept walking, her pace picking up as she neared an area where the wall disappeared and was replaced by a series of windows and metal frames. On the other side of the glass were dozens of people filling every single chair in the room. A few more were standing next to loved ones. Every person in the waiting area had a surgical mask on.

Adriana realized she was one of the few people in the building that didn't have one on and quickly dug into her backpack to grab a scarf. She wrapped it around her face as she reached the door and pulled it tight to create at least some kind of barrier against possible airborne illness.

She pushed through the door, using her elbow on the door handle to keep her hands sanitary, and stepped inside. A few people looked up at her and then returned their gazes to the floor along with all the others. Every forlorn pair of eyes looked as though they'd lost all hope.

Adriana wondered what these poor people were going through. Just a few days before, they had probably been happy, going about their lives as though nothing bad was ever going to happen. Then this.

She panned the room, doing her best not to meet anyone's gaze, and found a boy sitting in the corner. His blond hair was disheveled. He wore a blue T-shirt and a gray pair of shorts with white socks and matching sneakers with blue stripes.

The kid, it seemed, was there alone. The woman to his right sat next to a man who looked about her age, but they weren't paying any attention to the boy. To his left, just beyond a low end table with magazines on top of it was an older man with sagging, droopy eyes and thinning gray hair. Maybe that was his grandfather, but Adriana got a sad feeling that the boy was alone.

She walked across the room, doing her best to stay as quiet as possible despite the sound of the television in the corner. When she neared the boy, she stopped and bent her knees to lower herself to his level.

"Hello," she said, cocking her head to the side in a playful manner she hoped would disarm the boy's defenses.

He was staring down at the floor like most of the others. When she spoke to him, he looked up into her eyes with curiosity. "Hello," he said it more like a question than a greeting. "Who are you? You don't look like one of the doctors."

The boy spoke perfect English albeit with a thick Swedish accent.

Adriana let her broad grin narrow her eyes so the boy could see it despite the scarf over her mouth. "My name is Adriana," she said. "What's your name?"

The boy swallowed and looked her up and down, assessing whether or not she was dangerous. "Johan."

"Hello, Johan. It's nice to meet you. Are you here with your parents?"

The question caught the boy off guard. "No," he said, shaking his head timidly. "My dad..."

There was pain in his voice, and it was written in his eyes.

"What about your dad?"

"He's very sick."

She exhaled. While Adriana was as tough as nails, she also had a strong sense of empathy for those in suffering. She wished she could take their pain away, especially when it was children.

"Your dad got this flu that's going around?"

Johan nodded.

She noticed the people next to her were listening in on the conversation and decided it might be best if she and Johan had some privacy to continue talking. "Would it be okay if you step out into the hall with me? I'd like to help your dad if I can, but I need to ask you some questions."

The boy shrugged. "Sure."

He pushed himself up out of the chair and followed her to the door. Adriana held it open for him, letting him exit first. Then she allowed the door to close behind her as she stepped out into the corridor.

"Would you like something to drink?" she asked. "A Coke or something?"

He gave a weak nod.

"Good. Me, too."

She led the way around the corner to a couple of vending machines she'd noticed. Adriana stuffed her hand into her pocket and removed a credit card then slid it into the drink machine. "Coke, right?"

The boy nodded eagerly.

She pressed the button for a Coke, and a moment later a bottle clanked inside the contraption and rattled into the drawer at the bottom. Then she ran her card through the slider one more time and ordered a second Coke. When her bottle arrived at the bottom of the machine, she reached in through the plastic flap and removed both drinks, handing one to the grateful boy.

She twisted her lid off her drink and raised it to him. He gave an appreciative nod and took his cap off. After a few good swigs and some refreshed "ahhs" Adriana resumed her line of questioning.

"How long have you been here?"

"In the hospital?"

She nodded.

"Since yesterday. My dad got sick the night before after we got home from the football match."

The football match. There it was again. She knew that the popular theory was that ground zero for this outbreak centered around the football game between Sweden and Finland. Adriana had done her research on the flight over from France. The stadium, known as Malmö Stadion to most of the locals, held around twenty-six thousand people. The arena was a fairly average size by international standards, though growing up, Adriana had been accustomed to much larger venues in Madrid.

"So, you were at the match?" Adriana asked.

The boy stared down at the top of the bottle in his hands and nodded. "Yes. It was my first time getting to see the national team play."

Adriana wanted to give the boy a big hug, but she resisted. Instead, she tried to think of a gentle way of asking him more questions, but she also didn't want to pry so much that she upset the boy.

"Johan?"

The kid looked up at her. His weary eyes were red around the edges, but there was no sign that he was sick, no symptoms that the virus was ravaging his body. She was relieved at that, but Adriana also knew that his condition could, and likely would, change at any time.

"They've been giving your father medicine?" She already knew the answer but figured keeping the boy talking was a good thing. It also established a little goodwill that would hopefully make her next line of questions easier for him.

Johan nodded. "They've been trying lots of medicines, but nothing seems to work. There are a lot of other sick people here, too. Sometimes, I don't know if the doctors know what they're doing."

Adriana almost let out a laugh at that. Children were so innocent. From that innocence, brutal honesty sprouted forth and blossomed into some of the most hilarious things she'd ever heard. There were television shows based on such revelations. At the moment, though, she knew laughter wasn't appropriate.

During the training of her youth, Adriana had learned to fight, how to use weapons, and how to take down enemies that would do her harm. There was, however, another part of her training that had nothing to do with taking on those with evil intentions. This other portion of the learning process had to do with healing.

Desperate to cure the cancer ravaging his wife's body, Adriana's father had taken Adriana to a man who lived alone on a mountain in an old abandoned church. The place of worship looked more like an ancient fortress that had fallen prey to the battering of time and inattention.

When the two visitors had arrived in the ancient church, Adriana was surprised to see other people there. From a distance, the place appeared abandoned and in ruins. Yet the chapel remained largely intact. The stone floors were swept clean, curtains lined the windows, and there were a dozen beds lining the two walls.

Adriana noted a few of the patients as she walked by. There were no nurses, no doctors in lab coats or expensive machinery connected to those in the beds. At the front of the chapel, a man in gray robes sat in a simple wooden chair. Two candles burned on the floor next to him on either side.

As the two visitors approached, Adriana wondered if the guy was meditating. His gray robes looked like those of a monk. With his eyes closed and palms to the ceiling, the closer she got, the more she was convinced she was right about the meditation.

Adriana snapped back to the moment. Johan was staring up at her. The memory of her visit to the old church faded. Something inside her, however, begged her to revisit that day.

"Doctors do a good job," Adriana reassured the boy. "Sometimes, though, adults don't always have the answers."

She hated the way that sounded coming out of her mouth, and she could tell it did little to soothe the boy's pain.

She tousled his hair. "What was your favorite part of the match?" Adriana hoped a change of subject back to something the boy enjoyed would get things back on track.

He offered a faint grin. "The goals, I guess. It was exciting to see the best players from my country take on the best from another country. When the team scored, the crowd was the loudest thing I've ever heard in my life."

Adriana smiled at him and gave an understanding nod.

"The people were really funny," he said. "Some of them were saying words I didn't understand."

Adriana blurted a short laugh. "I can only imagine what you might have heard at a football game."

He thought for a second. "I thought the blimps were really cool, too."

Her forehead scrunched over her nose. "Blimps?"

"Yeah." The boy sounded moderately excited. "There were two radio-controlled blimps flying around. They sprayed a mist on the fans to cool them off. They didn't get to us, though." There was a hint of dejection in his voice. "So we went out to the restrooms and then the concession shops. I thought the blimps were cool, though. I've seen them drop prizes to people before but never spraying water on fans in the heat. It's a good idea, I think."

Adriana's mind kicked into another gear. Thoughts spun like gears in a sports car, revving at thousands of RPMs.

"Johan, would you mind taking me to see your father?"

The boy looked into her eyes, his own blue eyes droopy with sadness. "They said I have to wait in there."

"That's okay. Now that I'm here, they'll let you see him. Do you remember where he is?"

The boy nodded eagerly.

Adriana glanced around to make sure no one was listening. "Good. There's something I need to see."

12

MALMO

Adriana followed the boy through the hospital halls like a rat trying for cheese in a maze. There were several moments when Adriana wondered if the boy was lost. She had a feeling he was but didn't press the issue, though time was certainly critical.

They finally reached a room where the door was barely hanging open, leaving nothing but a crack between the frame and its front edge. Adriana noted the name on the plaque hanging next to the doorway.

"This is where your dad is?" she whispered.

Johan nodded and gently pushed the door open. Around the corner, all Adriana could see was the foot-end of the bed. She craned her neck first as the boy padded into the room. When the boy was out of sight, standing by his father's side, she picked up the chart hanging inside the door shelf and scanned over it.

The patient was exhibiting the same flu-like symptoms as everyone else. She was about to put the chart back when a voice froze her in place.

"Can I help you?"

Adriana turned and glanced over her shoulder. A woman in a

white lab coat with wavy blonde hair pulled back in a ponytail was standing ten feet away. She had her hands in her pockets.

"Actually, yes," Adriana said, relieved the woman spoke English. "You're a doctor here, correct?"

The woman nodded and approached the door. "Yes. I'm Dr. Forsberg. Are you a friend or relative of this patient?"

"Friend," Adriana said quickly, a little too quickly for her liking, so she hurriedly moved the conversation to her question. "I was wondering...what time did you receive the first patients coming in with this illness?"

The doctor stopped a few feet away and took the chart from Adriana. "A few days ago. Surely you've seen the news. You should probably be wearing a mask, by the way." She didn't sound happy, borderline irritated.

"Yes, you're right. I'll be sure to get one on my way out."

"Might as well stay. You'll probably end up here in the next twenty-four hours."

"Thanks for the tip. My question, though: I wasn't talking about the day. I'm more interested in the time between the first arrivals and my friend here."

The doctor frowned. "Difficult to say. I think the first victims were..." She ran her eyes down the chart, checking some of the information. Then she tapped the clipboard. "Yes, he was one of the earlier ones, but it looks like he came in around four hours after our first patients, though I'm going from memory on the others. That's a strange question. Are you some kind of investigator?"

Adriana considered the question. She couldn't tell the doctor the truth: that she was working for a covert anti-terrorist agency. Then again, if she wanted to get every ounce of information she could, maybe it was time to use a little empowerment with the doctor.

She glanced down the hall in both directions and then pulled the doctor aside, as if about to share a secret.

"I am," Adriana confessed. "And I am trying to figure out if this epidemic was an attack or simply nature taking its course."

The doctor's face suddenly expressed concern. "An attack?"

Adriana put a finger to her lips and shushed the woman. "Keep it down. The last thing we want to do is incite a panic."

She could tell sharing this with the doctor had created the desired effect. The woman was all too eager to help now.

"I need to know the exact time your first patient came in with these symptoms."

Dr. Forsberg's brow wrinkled, and her eyes narrowed as she considered the question. "Six in the morning, two days ago."

"You're sure?"

"Of course, I'm sure. You don't forget something like that."

"I would think someone coming in with the flu might be somewhat common."

Forsberg snorted. "Flu, sure. But not the kind that kills patients that were previously healthy and strong."

Adriana's mind flashed back to the stories her grandparents told her, the ones about healthy people being killed during the Spanish pandemic.

"The first patient died?" Adriana asked, now realizing that the woman had used the word *victim* before.

"Yes. Just this morning. Patient zero expired a few hours ago along with two others. I'm afraid they're only the first of many if we can't find a way to fight whatever this virus is."

Adriana thought hard, her mind racing. She sighed and glanced back into the room where Johan was standing next to the bed. She noticed movement over her shoulder and saw a woman approaching. The lady wore tight jeans and a white T-shirt. Her disheveled dirty-blonde hair cascaded over her shoulders and looked like it hadn't been washed or brushed in a few days.

The woman was carrying a cup of coffee and excused herself with a feeble grin as she passed Adriana and Dr. Forsberg, making her way into the room.

That must have been Johan's mother, at least as best as Adriana could figure.

"Thank you for your time, Doctor," Adriana said. "I need to speak to them for a moment."

The doctor shrugged and crossed her arms. "They're under a tremendous amount of stress right now. I don't know how much longer he has to live."

"Which is why it's vital that I speak with them."

"Fine," Forsberg relented. "I'll give you two minutes. Then I'm calling security."

"I am security."

Adriana let the sentence hang in the hall as she spun and strode into the room.

Her head flooded with memories of the old church where her father had introduced her to the healer. She saw Johan's father lying on his back in the bed. His face was pale with huge red circles around the eyes. She imagined the man was strong, rugged, even attractive before this illness had struck and ravaged his body.

The mother was sitting in a chair next to the window, sipping her coffee, cradling the cup with both hands like it was the last java on Earth.

"Hello," Adriana said in a hushed tone. "My name is Adriana."

"Who are you?"

"I'm here to help you."

She flashed back to the church, the chapel where the beds lined the walls. She recalled that some of the patients were hooked up to intravenous tubes with bags of various-colored liquids dripping through needles plunged into their wrists. While the building was clearly a chapel, it also bore the distinct look of a hospital, though it was unlike any she'd ever seen.

The machines weren't the most modern, not like the ones she'd witnessed in other hospitals. Some beeped, others wheezed, but the patients seemed to be comfortable, all in various states of differing treatments.

The man in the gray robes had stood next to her, pointing to a patient with reddish bags under his eyes. His ashen skin indicated an illness that had drawn his energy, plunging him into a state of weakness and dehydration. He was the visage of death incarnate, yet he still breathed, his chest rising and falling slowly, deliberately, pulling air into his lungs without strain. The young girl had stared at the man before turning to face the gray-robed figure. His eyes were concealed by the hood hanging over his head.

"What's wrong with him?" young Adriana had asked.

"What do you think is wrong with him?"

The girl shrugged. "He looks sick."

"Yes?"

The response urged her to continue her assessment. She'd just met this man a few minutes before, and now he was asking her for her diagnosis? She was just a girl. "I don't know. I guess maybe he has the flu." She said the last sentence more as a question than statement.

"Correct," the monk affirmed. "He has contracted a very aggressive form of the flu virus."

"Shouldn't he be at a hospital?"

The monk's lips curled into a wry grin. His eyes squinted in the shadow of the hood, stretching out the skin on his cheeks. "What do you think this place is, child?"

Adriana looked around. "A church."

"It is a place of healing, both spiritual and physical. Do you know that the universe is only made of two things?"

The question caught the young girl off guard. "That doesn't sound right."

"But it is." The monk's accent was difficult to place. She thought maybe German, perhaps Eastern European. "Everything you see, touch, smell, taste in the universe is made of either matter or energy."

"If you say so."

"Much of the world's medical field only addresses one, the matter. Here, we treat both."

"Both?"

"Yes. One cannot have good matter without good energy."

She didn't understand where he was going with all this.

"How does that help this guy with the flu?" Adriana asked.

"It allows us to open our minds to other possibilities for healing, possibilities outside the realm of what modern medicine teaches."

"So...is he going to be okay?" Adriana flashed a glance over at the sick man.

"He already is, my child."

"What did you do?"

The grin on the monk's face stretched a few millimeters farther. "You can see on that piece of paper over there."

Adriana turned and looked to the nightstand next to the bed. A sheet of old paper rested on the surface. She stepped over to it and started reading. It looked more like a grocery list, though she didn't know what kind of store would carry such things.

"What is all this?" she asked.

"Sometimes, the simple answers are the correct ones. While much of the world relies on synthetic compounds for treatment of diseases, we understand there is a much more ancient and elegant solution to such matters."

He motioned to another section of the room, cordoned off by a stone wall that seemed like it didn't belong. The concrete blocks didn't match the rest of the ancient stone composing the rest of the building. Glass windows occupied much of the inward-facing façade. Inside, four people in similar gray robes, faces covered in surgical masks, heads bearing bluish hats, and hands gloved, hovered over modern machinery and lab equipment. Beakers hung from metal clasps long the far wall; other items she recognized from labs in doctors' offices were positioned in varying spots on counters around the room. A centrifuge was one she immediately identified, vials of blood filling round slots within.

Adriana returned to the topic at hand, holding off more questions about the lab for later. "What would make these ingredients more powerful than modern medicine?"

The monk grinned broadly. "My child, not all things are always what they seem. Did you know that your modern medicine is also mimicked by something called the Placebo Effect?"

She didn't recall hearing anything about that. "No. What is that?"

"Every pill ever produced is tested against a placebo, or sugar pill. In almost every test ever conducted, 30 percent of subjects produced the same results with a sugar pill as with the actual medicine."

Adriana couldn't believe it. "How is that possible?"

The monk continued. "We don't know all the secrets of the universe, but one seems to stand out in the open for all to see." He put his hands out wide, displaying the room once more. "We are surrounded by two things, energy and matter. Sometimes, simply believing you are experiencing healing or relief from symptoms is enough to change the energy. When you change the energy, you take away the source of the illness that displays itself as matter. The two are intertwined, connected in an elegant, scientific dance."

Adriana scrunched her forehead, processing the information. She was only a young child but had a keen ability to understand things other kids her age, even older, could not.

"Is that what that compound does, the one on the paper?" She pointed at the sheet.

"In a way," he said. "It treats the energy of a patient, but it also has powerful compounds that are capable of combating aggressive viruses." He motioned to the little concrete-and-glass lab off to the side. "We study many different biological threats here. It is how we take care of our...people."

People? What did he mean by that? She let that question go, assuming, for a moment, that he meant the citizens of the nearby town. Adriana's hopes grew. "Can it cure cancer?" She thought of her mother in all her suffering.

The monk's face grew long, crestfallen. He knew about the girl's familial struggle but didn't let on. "Sadly, my child, it cannot. This particular medicine was created for viruses. There could, however, exist a combination of elements that could eliminate cancer. Perhaps someday you will be the one to find it."

There was no disguising her pain, but she pushed through and asked one more question. "If this recipe can eliminate certain illnesses, why hide it here? Why not take it out into the world and help people everywhere?"

His face remained stoic, touched with a hint of sadness. "Because, Adriana, the world is not ready for it yet. They would rather simply believe that the big companies are giving them what is best, that the governments are only approving things that will help people, when the truth couldn't be further away."

He nodded to her. "Take note of those ingredients. You may need them someday. It is to be made into a kind of tea. The natural ingredients in it will fight viruses in the human body and keep the immune system from trying to do too much." The monk didn't tell her at that moment why he was giving her such a gift. It wouldn't be until she was a teenager that her father revealed the true nature of this place. It was a hospital for an ancient sect of warriors, similar to the Shinobi, some of the most powerful warriors of days long gone, or so the world was led to believe.

Adriana recalled the things her grandparents said about the Spanish influenza pandemic and how so many had died as a direct result of their immune systems going haywire and attacking good cells as well as the virus. According to this monk, the recipe he possessed could prevent something like that from happening again.

"Where did you get this?" she asked out of curiosity, doing her best not to be disrespectful.

He chuckled. "My grandfather created it," he said. "He was one of the survivors of the influenza pandemic and swore he wouldn't rest until he created something that could fight most of the known viruses of the time, as well as those that could come in the future. It took him many years to discover it. Viruses are a peculiar organism, especially influenza. They are capable of mutating, changing to become more powerful, more adept at resisting many treatments. To combat such a virus, we needed to use both the best of what modern medicine could offer as well as our own ancient techniques. He was ahead of, and behind, his time."

The old man moved closer to her, gliding across the floor as if floating. "Keep it safe, my child. For the things that can create life can also be made to take it."

The young Adriana nodded and glanced back to the faded sheet of paper. "Why? Why give it to me? I'm just a girl."

He passed her a comforting smile, one that also bore a subtle hint of empowerment. "Because, Adriana, the day may come when you will need it. And perhaps there could come a time when you may need to share it with the world."

Adriana stared at Johan's father as she recalled the events from her childhood. The old monk had been right. The sick man started recovering later that day. She remembered seeing him the following morning. The guy was up and walking around, eating like a horse, and even laughing.

The list of ingredients propped themselves in front of her mind's eye. Perhaps that was the reason for the experience with the monk. Was that possible? She'd let go of the notion of coincidence long ago. Maybe the monk's concoction would work here, though there was more than an ounce of doubt in her heart.

"Here," she said and moved to a table on the right under a cabinet. A pen was lying next to a notepad. She picked it up and started scribbling. "Get these things and some hot water. Put these ingredients into the water and let them sit for five minutes. Then have him drink."

The mother frowned as she looked over at the piece of paper. "What? Who are you?"

"I'm here to help."

"He can't drink anything. He won't keep it down."

Adriana leveled her gaze at Johan's mother. Her eyes drooped over the surgical mask covering her mouth and nose. "Trust me," Adriana said. "This will work."

The woman took the paper from Adriana's fingers and stared at it.

"There's...a grocery store nearby that might have these things." She looked up at the visitor again. "I don't understand how any of this will help."

"What's the worst thing that can happen? It won't hurt to try."

The woman nodded and averted her eyes back to the paper. When she looked up again to ask another question, Adriana was gone.

Johan's mother turned her gaze to her son. "Johan, do you know her?"

The boy nodded.

"Who is she?"

The boy's eyes never flinched as he stared at his mother. "An angel."

13

LYON

June paced the war room. She'd been back and forth between there and the main control room all morning and into the afternoon. The computers were running as many checks as they could from footage around the Middle East, but so far nothing had turned up a positive ID on any of the subjects.

She was beginning to lose hope when the phone in her pocket started ringing.

"Go ahead." Her answer to the call was straight to the point.

"We have a match," the young woman on the other end said.

"I'll be right there."

June ended the call and hurried out the door and into the corridor. She flew down the hall, doing her best not to run, like a child scurrying around a pool after being told no running.

She burst through the doors at the end of the hall and stepped onto the floor of the main control room. A young woman with curly brown hair waved to her from behind a row of computers. Two more members their team—a skinny man with thick dark hair and a woman with short blonde curls—were hovering over her shoulders.

June walked around the end of the workstation and craned her neck to get a better view of the screen. Her heart skipped a beat the second she saw the two images.

"That's him. That's our informant."

There on the monitor, two younger men were walking with an older man. His head was covered in a blond wig, and the facial hair he'd donned before was gone, but June would have recognized that face anywhere. The long, drooped nose, the wrinkles, the sagging cheeks—none of it slipped by her.

"We weren't able to get an ID on him, but we figured if we nailed these two then we'd find your guy." The woman at the computer pointed to the two images of the younger men in the corner. "They don't have any known terrorist connections. Criminal records didn't turn up much. A few minor crimes but nothing serious."

"They were easy to recruit," June said. "Guys who are down on their luck, maybe who've dabbled in a few illegal activities. Nothing to lose." She scanned their information faster than the other team members could relay it. "Where are they?"

"This image was taken at the airport in Brussels."

"Brussels? So, they didn't take more precautions?"

"No, ma'am." It was the young man's turn to speak up. "They must have believed they were in the clear once they were two countries away. They got careless."

"Or they wanted us to find them." June put the possibility out there even though she didn't really buy it.

The other three glanced at each other with unease.

"You think that's the case?" the woman standing next to her asked.

"No," June confessed. "But we need to be prepared for anything. The old man in that picture is extremely clever. He destroyed my outfit's headquarters." She was tempted to let them in on the theory about the influenza outbreak in Sweden, but for the time being she decided that was on a need-to-know basis. And at the moment, they didn't need to know. "He's capable of much worse than that. As things stand, every major civilian population center is a target. So, where did those three go?"

"We've gone over the passenger manifests to double-check. They flew to Prague, we assume to board a connecting flight somewhere."

"Prague?" June asked.

"Yes, that's correct."

The three team members stared at June, waiting for her to make a decision.

She knew what they wanted to know.

"Get a unit in that airport. Do it quietly. The last thing I want to do is for this guy to know that we've found him and are watching."

"Beg your pardon, ma'am. They've already gone."

"Gone?"

June leaned forward and looked at the screen.

"Yes," the young woman said. "Those three men boarded a plane heading to Baku two days ago."

June rubbed her head again and spun around. She wanted to scream, but she knew that wouldn't fly. She had to remain professional, composed, collected. Leaders didn't panic. They were only a few steps behind the Teacher, but that could make a huge difference. She was foolish to think these terrorists would be hanging around in the Czech Republic, or anywhere else for that matter. Of course they had fled as quickly as possible.

Baku. The picturesque capital of Azerbaijan was a place where men like the Teacher could find allies. He could be anywhere now. June had a creeping feeling that they had missed their opportunity, if it had ever truly presented itself.

"What can we get out of Baku?" June asked, already fairly certain of the answer.

"We might be able to get some assistance out of their police, but it could take time." The young man answered the question before the other two could.

"See what you can find out," June ordered.

The man took a phone out of his pocket and stepped away, already making calls to see what he could scrounge up on the Azerbaijan front.

June had been in tough spots before. This one, however, was challenging every ounce of wit she could muster.

"Director?" The young agent put his phone against the opposite palm to silence the microphone. June spun around. "We have someone in Baku who can help us."

Some good news for a change.

"Make it happen. I need to know where those three went."

The young man got back on the phone while sitting down in an empty chair across the aisle. He furiously wrote down several details on a piece of paper and then ended the call.

He stood up and returned to the other two team members and began issuing orders. His contact in Baku needed the images they'd been studying as well as the possible aliases these three were using. It was highly likely they had multiple identities, but more than two per person might be overly cautious. June doubted the villains had gone to those lengths. Even those most cunning bad guys slipped up.

"Cross-reference any names on the flight from Brussels that also flew out of Baku. I want seat locations for every person on any flight going to the Middle East."

June grinned at the young man's command. He was, no doubt, a good investigator for Pavard. Perhaps he would fit in with her unit—if he was interested. She did, after all, have a few openings. The thought hit her in the gut, and she mustered enough grit to push the pain aside.

The two young women took notes in a flurry of activity. Then the group split up, leaving the woman with the dark curls at her computer. Her fingers flew across the keyboard.

June had one thought. It kept pulsing in the front of her mind. She could see the Teacher's face, the smug look in his eyes as he stood there in the Shadow Cell headquarters, watching as the bombs hit targets that meant nothing to him.

He'd gotten away, but she was closing in. The Teacher could only run and hide for so long before June tightened the noose, eventually choking him out.

14

MALMO

Adriana stepped up to the stadium gate with a surgical mask over her face and a badge in her hand. The guard stared at the identification for a moment then shook his head.

There were dozens of police cars around the parking area. Tape cordoned off many of the gates where ordinary fans normally entered. She was no fan and certainly had no intention of going in through one of the usual entrances. Adriana was there to find something, and she knew that if it was there it would likely be down under the stadium somewhere.

"Listen," she said to the cop, "you can either let me in so I can do my job and investigate what caused this outbreak, or you can explain to your boss why you didn't let a person with one of these into the stadium and allowed millions of innocent people to die."

The guard's blond eyebrows furrowed beneath his tanned forehead as he gazed at the ID card. He'd probably never seen one with such a high rank from Interpol before, which only confused him more. The guy decided it wasn't worth the trouble and stepped aside, motioning her though.

Adriana gave a curt nod as she hurried through the entrance. "Thank you."

She made her way into the underbelly of the arena, down a ramp to the tunnels that ran along the ground level all the way around the field's perimeter. Adriana paused at the bottom and took a quick look in both directions. The tunnels looked the same, with cinder block walls, concrete floors, and exposed ventilation ducts running along the ceiling. Pipes of various sizes were also visible, along with gauges and levers she figured were almost never touched, except by engineers making sure things were working properly.

Adriana cut to the right, figuring there was difference. She'd end up in the same place either way if she didn't find anything. It was a long shot; that much she knew. There likely wouldn't be any trace of what she was trying to find, but she had to try.

Walking through the tunnels, she passed several cops as well as people in suits who were clearly there to investigate the possibility that the stadium was the epicenter of the outbreak. She was surprised that security hadn't been tighter up above, which caused her to believe that the government was taking the stadium theory far less seriously than the media.

Adriana raised her badge and nodded to the group of investigators as she strode by, doing her best not to make too much eye contact but enough so they wouldn't get suspicious. Some of the people were in hazmat gear, which she found peculiar. Most were only wearing the same kind of mask she had covering her face.

She started to think maybe she needed one of those suits, but it was too late now. If the disease was airborne, she'd have contracted it at the hospital.

The tunnel made a sharp, angled turn to the left, straightened out for a short distance, and then cut left again. She'd reached the end of the arena. Adriana scanned the walls and doors on both sides, but nothing stood out—certainly not what she was looking for.

She sighed and kept moving. Nothing was ever easy.

Down the length of the next section of tunnel, several more cops and investigators were checking some of the pipes. One engineer was turning a valve, releasing pressure in one of the long metal tubes. Adriana noted one of the hazmat suits had the letters WHO emblazoned in a blue logo and letters on the left breast, the signature matching light blue lines ran vertical and horizontal, intersecting in the center of the chest.

Again, she thought it interesting that these researchers were in full gear, complete with respirators, while the rest of the teams were equipped with nothing but surgical masks. The worry she'd felt before swelled inside her, but she kept moving, striding by the group surrounding the pipes and valve, hoping they wouldn't stop her.

One of the cops gave her a stoic gaze but then returned his attention to the engineer working on the valve hanging from the wall.

She hurried along, doing her best not to look like she was in a hurry, and reached the other end of the arena tunnel. She noticed another ramp much like the one she'd descended a few minutes before. It rose gradually to another parking area on the opposite side of the stadium from where she'd parked her car. At the top, a pair of guards kept watch over the entrance.

Just like before, the tunnel veered to the left at an angle, heading toward the north end of the field. Adriana desperately wanted to get out of sight from the crew she'd just passed. The more people who saw her, the more likely trouble would follow.

She was about to round the next corner when she noticed a door hanging slightly ajar. Through the crack she could see some soccer goals, though they weren't regulation size. The netting and connected posts were the smaller, foldable kind she'd seen kids using on short fields. She'd even seen them used in drills for older players. Her immediate thought was that the room must have been primarily for storage, but a little voice inside her suggested she should have a look. What could it hurt, right?

Adriana stole a quick glance back over her shoulder. The cops and people in the hazmat suits were still occupied with whatever the engineer was checking. How many people did it take to turn a valve? No wonder governments were so inefficient.

She shook off the thought and peeled the door open a little wider, sliding through the gap and into the room. She eased the door shut again, keeping it ajar as it had been when she found it, and then looked around.

The storage space stretched fifteen feet to the ceiling, ran at least fifty feet in length, and was thirty feet across. Her initial assessment of the room being used for storage was spot on. There were bags of soccer balls, small goals used for halftime entertainment or drills, stacks of cones, boxes piled on top of one another at the far end of the room, equipment bags, plastic cases, corner flags, and dozens of other random soccer-related equipment.

The two items that instantly caught her attention, however, were two bulbous white objects along the exterior wall. Most of the air had been released from the bladders, but there was no mistaking what they were. The two blimps were still half-full of air, sitting silently on the floor, one end abutted to the other. She looked back over her shoulder and listened for a few seconds. The sounds of the people talking halfway down the tunnel echoed into the room, but they weren't getting any closer and there were no sounds of footsteps approaching.

Adriana tiptoed across the floor and stopped short of the two miniature blimps. The things were designed to look like replicas of modern blimps, though the twin fans at the front and back were positioned differently than most dirigibles she'd seen.

Two white metal pipes jutted out from the faux cockpit and passenger cabin in the center of the aircraft. Adriana stepped closer and lifted the sagging portion of the fabric so she could get a better look at the cylinders.

She bent one knee and crouched down, still holding up the deflated fabric. Sure enough, there were tiny little holes drilled into the pipes, offset on either side to deliver a fine mist in both directions.

These were the blimps Johan was talking about, unless there were others somewhere in the stadium. *Unlikely*.

Adriana was careful not to touch the metal rods jutting out from under the blimp's carriage. While she figured any virus that may have still been sitting around was likely long dead, she preferred not to risk it. She had a peripheral understanding about how long most bacteria and viruses could survive in the open, but she also had the feeling she'd learned some could make it longer than others once exposed to the elements of air, variable temperatures, and humidity.

If the Red Ring operatives responsible for this attack—assuming that's what it was—had managed to sneak these devices into the stadium, why would they be so careless as to leave them behind?

The answer, she decided in the blink of an eye, was that the blimps were too large to simply carry out of the arena. They were bulky and awkward. On top of that, even if all the air had been drained from the bladders, which would take considerable time, it would take even more time to pack them up for transport.

No, if the terrorists had used these for a biological attack, leaving the dirigibles behind was the smart move as long as there was no evidence on them such as fingerprints or some kind of DNA. She doubted either would be discovered on the two blimps. That would be too easy. Not to mention even if there were such evidence, it would take forever to get confirmation of the identities.

She needed to know for sure if the virus had been delivered through these blimps and if so, how the terrorists were able to get access to this area and to the radio-controlled units.

Adriana let out a long exhale. She was going to have to use the local talent for this one. There was no other choice.

Working with local authorities came fraught with its own set of problems. She could easily poke her head out of the door and ask the people down the corridor to come check out what she had found. That, however, would bring questions. Who was she? Why was she here? What did she want?

She could flash her Interpol badge Pavard had issued, and that would solve some of the problems, but more questions would follow. And using the badge would bring resistance from cops she figured didn't always like working with international or federal police.

Then again, WHO was already here conducting an investigation, so the odds the locals would be more willing to work with her had to be significantly higher.

Reluctantly, Adriana walked over to the door and nudged it open.

She took another deep breath and exhaled before she waved toward the group of cops and WHO investigators.

“Hey,” she said, knowing the term would get the attention of not only Swedes who used it as a greeting, but of the international team from the World Health Organization.

15

MALMO

Adriana pulled out her cell phone, standing outside in the tunnel just far enough away to feel like she wasn't in the way of the investigators, but also close enough that she could see through the open doorway at what they were doing.

A team from the CDC had joined the people from WHO and had moved everyone not wearing a protective suit out of the storage room as they began working to figure out what was inside the rods sticking out from under the blimp.

Adriana pressed the green call button on her screen and put the phone to her ear. It only took two rings before June answered on the other end.

"What's the story?"

"It's getting interesting."

"Yeah. How so?"

"Well, I think I found what they used to spread this virus."

"Really?" June sounded more surprised than she had intended.

Adriana continued staring through the open doorway. "Yeah. They used a couple of novelty blimps; radio controlled. I've seen these kinds of things before at games. They drop prizes on the fans below. These, apparently, were equipped with a more lethal cargo."

One of the men in the CDC gear twisted the last screw with his screwdriver. He set the tool aside and began prying open the miniature cabin. The bomb squad had already been in and investigated. X-rays of the box attached to the blimp showed there were no explosives inside, only multiple bladders and pumps with tubes running out to the delivery rods.

“They crop-dusted the fans at the soccer game. Sprayed the virus down onto them.”

June took a deep breath on the other end of the line and loudly exhaled. “That’s awful.”

“Yeah. It really is.”

“You okay?”

“I’m fine. I was chatting with one of the CDC guys, and they said that they believe it isn’t airborne.”

Adriana believed them, which made the use of hazmat suits by the investigators that much more perplexing. She figured they played things on the safe side. Working for WHO and the CDC required the utmost diligence and caution. One slipup and things could get bad quickly. She’d heard stories about some of the diseases that were kept in lockdown in the Atlanta headquarters of the Centers for Disease Control. Much of it sounded like a science fiction novel or alien conspiracy theories about Area 51. It was hard to know what was truth and what was exaggerated or wild, tinfoil-hat-driven fantasy.

Some of the stuff she’d heard, however, was downright scary. There had to be some truth to it, at least in part. Security around the building was beyond tight. Like a maximum-security high-tech prison. They were definitely protecting the public from something bad in there. What it was, Adriana could only speculate.

“They sure about that?” June asked.

Adriana unconsciously took a step back. “Yeah.” She hid the doubt in her mind. “Looks like they’re about to collect samples.”

The investigators pulled glass vials out of their gear bags. They scraped the inside of the now-open cabin and then inserted the tools into the vials, sealed them, and then repeated the process.

“What’s the situation on the ground there with the population?”

"The people are sick, violently so."

"I saw that the first victims died a few hours ago."

Adriana's heart thumped once, a painful knife digging into it as she thought about poor Johan and his father. She'd given the boy's mother an antidote. Whether it would work and save the man, Adriana wasn't sure. It was the same concoction the healer had given her decades before when she was just a little girl learning the ways of self-preservation in all its many facets.

Johan's mother may not have even gone out to get the ingredients. Adriana wouldn't blame the woman. Why should she trust some stranger that showed up in her husband's room with her son in tow and offered a mysterious brew that could eradicate this powerful strain of influenza?

In hindsight, Adriana wondered if she would have believed her had the roles been reversed, prior esoteric wisdom aside.

"Yes, I heard a few of them expired." Adriana used the term not out of callousness or a lack of empathy. Saying they expired made it seem less real, more like a story she was reading in third person that didn't have any effect on her life. She couldn't let the deaths of innocent people interfere with what she had to do, as horrible as that sounded. "Hopefully, they can come up with something that works soon."

The antibiotics the hospitals were using had, thus far, shown little effect on the virus that was raging through the population. And from what Adriana heard in passing, the illness was spreading rapidly through the country. She'd overheard one person say that a few people were sick in Copenhagen. It wouldn't be long before that city was overtaken by the outbreak. Then the region would fall next. Borders would be closed between the nations of Europe. Then the Middle East and Asia would follow suit.

Adriana imagined the suddenness of all this, the mass hysteria that would ensue, if it hadn't already. Based on what she'd seen at the hospital earlier, it wouldn't be long before people started panicking.

"I guess they'll be scrambling to figure out an antivirus," June said, cutting into Adriana's thoughts.

"That's the plan, but by then thousands of people could be dead. Maybe more." Adriana thought about the tea recipe she'd given Johan's mother. It was a long shot, but maybe...just maybe it would work.

"You're okay, right? You're not experiencing any symptoms?"

Adriana shook her head. "No. I'm fine." She quickly changed the subject. "Got anything on your end?"

"Not much so far, but we're making progress."

"You don't sound happy about it."

"I'm not. Every minute we waste is another minute these terrorists could be planning their next attack. They could even be going forward with the next one, which is why we need to hurry."

"What do you have?"

June paused for a second. "We know they flew out of Brussels."

"Belgium?"

"Yep. Apparently, they took a boat to Dunkirk, then crossed the border into Belgium and flew out, probably later that day."

"You know where they went?" Adriana didn't get her hopes up.

"Baku, Azerbaijan."

Adriana knew the city. She'd been there before. It was a jewel on the Caspian Sea, full of unique Arabian architecture with a flair of modern design.

"Nice spot," Adriana quipped.

"I doubt they went for the beaches. If I had to guess, they're long gone by now."

"And that's why you sound grumpy. You don't know where they went from there."

"Is it that obvious?"

Adriana rolled her shoulders and let out a short chuckle. "Kind of."

"Well, at any rate, we have someone in Baku who is looking into it."

"Interpol guy?"

"I believe so, although Pavard's team didn't clarify that point. Now that you mention it, maybe he's not officially on the payroll."

"Sounds like you've got everything under control there."

"You're funny. Get that smart mouth from your boyfriend?"

"Could be. What's the next move?" Adriana got back to business.

"As soon as you figure something out in Sweden, let me know. You may need to rendezvous with the man in Baku, but that will all depend."

Adriana knew what she meant. It all depended on timing. Two days from now, the guy in Baku would likely be of little help. Time was critical right now. And every second that passed only raised the potential for more attacks.

One of the cops Adriana passed before rounded the corner and was walking straight toward her. He stared at her with dead eyes as he approached.

"Okay, thanks for the info. I have to go. I'll be in touch when I find anything else."

"Sounds good."

Adriana ended the call and slipped the phone into her pocket as the cop stopped in front of her.

"Well?" she asked, doing nothing to hide the expectation in her voice.

The cop nodded and spoke in a heavy Swedish accent. "You need to see this."

16

BAKU, AZERBAIJAN

Imad Rashid sat at the little workstation in the front corner of his dark studio apartment. Thick curtains concealed the two windows at the other end of the room, blocking out most of the bright sunlight from the clear sky beyond. Except it was already night. The sun had gone down hours ago.

He'd lost track of time, working on a project for a friend out of Lyon. Imad didn't necessarily work for Interpol on the record. He preferred to be on more of a contract-only basis with them.

It wasn't that he didn't trust Interpol. Well, for the most part he trusted them. But any organization that was run by a government, or multiple governments, was something he feared. Those kinds of entities, after all, could be easily swayed by the temptations of corruption. Corruption led to people getting eliminated and in more than one way.

Imad preferred to keep things simple. It was the way he had always operated. One look around his modest apartment would reflect that. He wasn't a minimalist, though, as his Ferrari 488 Spider in the garage downstairs would attest. He simply chose where to be indulgent and where to keep things uncomplicated.

He avoided relationships like an infectious disease—appropriate, he thought, considering that seemed to be a very real concern at the moment.

Imad followed the news religiously. He had three computer monitors attached to the wall behind his desk, two for keeping up with breaking news updates or things going on in the world, the third for his actual work. From time to time, he'd need more than one monitor for a project, but the one he was presently working on didn't require such intricate systems. Not yet anyway.

He knew the media around the entire planet was corrupt and spreading lies, no matter their political alliance. Imad made it his business to put the truth out there. He leaked information to a list of websites whose owners regularly posted content from the real world, not the fabricated stuff passing across his screens all the time.

The main reason Imad followed the news outlets so closely was so he could dissect what they were saying, find the truth behind it, and then put that out there for the world to consume. Sooner or later —he hoped—people would figure out it was time for a change in how they received their information.

That wasn't to say his activist mentality was the only reason he watched the news.

There were, on occasion, a few rare moments when they actually reported things that were going on as they happened, without spinning the stories or trying to make more out of things than they were.

This wasn't one of those times.

The monitor on the left was scrolling a story across a red ticker at the bottom of the screen about a new influenza outbreak in Saint Petersburg in Russia. He squinted at the screen for a second and then returned his attention to the one in the center.

Imad already knew something like this was going to happen. He didn't have a ton of medical knowledge, but everything that was transpiring in Sweden, and now Denmark and Finland, wasn't some random incident. It was clearly some kind of biological attack. That, or someone messed up.

He'd considered the latter, but the series of facts continued to point toward something more deliberate, more sinister. People responsible for protecting powerful viruses had fail-safes upon fail-safes in place. If someone was transporting a new superbug they'd discovered, it was highly unlikely the virus would manage to escape on its own, or by accident.

His contact at Interpol hadn't been too forthcoming with the information regarding the three men they were looking for, but Imad didn't need him to be. He connected the dots on his own.

Three men, two of them younger, the third an older man with a long, peppered beard. While his Interpol contact hadn't said they were terrorists, Imad already knew. The initial images he received were from traffic cameras on the streets of Liverpool, right before and after the bombings took place.

He retraced the footage, scanning the faces of the men who got out of the car in front of the SUV carrying the older man. The images were taken in rapid succession, and he flipped through them like an old cartoon book until he found one that showed a glimpse of the old man's face along with those of the two men springing him from captivity.

Imad frowned then stretched a square around the faces with a few clicks and drags of the computer mouse. The selected space enlarged and zoomed closer.

"Hello there," Imad said in a muted tone.

His cat on the couch nearby perked up its head and then a few seconds later returned to its nap.

"I don't think I've seen you three before."

Imad clicked a few other places on the screen and then zoomed in closer. "Nope. Definitely haven't seen you three before."

He cropped the images, saved them, and then dragged the new files into an application he had acquired a few years before. He preferred the term *borrowed*, though he'd actually stolen the app from a US-based tech company that was pitching it to the government for a big contract.

In the end, the feds went with someone else, but the program worked perfectly. Apparently, the startup wanted too much money for it. When Imad discovered the CEO shopping it around on the global market, he jumped on it. Smuggling a download from the underground of digital goods wasn't a difficult thing. He often found it humorous that hackers and shady characters who spent so much time trying not to get caught would be so careless with their wares. He'd procured the application without detection and then dipped out of the marketplace within minutes, sending false signals to a dozen other locations in case they tried to trace where the program went.

They never found him. He knew they never would. If there was a *they*. Any hit men or hired guns would search Moscow, New York, San Francisco, and several other places before giving up the fruitless quest. The last place they would think to look would be Baku.

He made sure the search protocols were in place and then hit the Run button. Then Imad laced his fingers on the top of his head and leaned back in his chair to relax and let the computer do the work.

The hard part, as far as he was concerned, was done. Getting the images from databases in England was more difficult, even with certain permissions granted by Interpol.

Now, he could simply let his sweet software do the heavy lifting.

It was loosely based on sky-tracking software the United States had developed in the 1990s, but it was so much more powerful now. Face Lock, as it was touted by the original developer, could identify more than a hundred thousand facial details and differentiate them from others that the naked eye would consider a spot-on match.

Not only was the application powerful at an unprecedented level, it was also faster than anything else on the planet. Imad still wondered, from time to time, why the United States government had decided to go with something else. That government, along with dozens more, were all too happy to spend hundreds of millions of dollars on a jet fighter, but heaven forbid they drop ten or twenty on a piece of software that could make the world safer and do a better job than any of its competitors.

Oh well. Their loss was Imad's gain, and he was more than okay with that.

He watched as the two peripheral screens switched over to join the search and began flashing images in the center, then moved them to the corners as they identified potential matches from every airport within the region and even beyond. The pictures blinked so rapidly that he couldn't even get a good look at the people the application was eliminating or flagging as matches.

Imad stood up and turned toward the cat. His pet was still asleep on the couch, resting comfortably on a windbreaker. He shook his head. Some people said that cats were useless animals. Moments like this caused him to agree a little, though he still loved his kitty. The love he felt from that cat and the love he shared, Imad thought, made them useful.

He wandered around the couch and reached over the back, tousling the fur on the animal's head before walking into the kitchen and opening the refrigerator. He pulled out a Coke and twisted the lid, then took a swig. Imad put the bottle back in the fridge and stepped over to the covered windows. He pulled back one of the curtains and looked out into the city.

There wasn't much to see on his street. The songs calling people to prayer had died off long ago, giving way to the eerie silence of night. There were places in Baku where a decent nightlife could be found, but he preferred to stay home. Imad was kind of a loner in that regard. The city offered plenty of bars and clubs for people to meet and socialize, but he'd grown tired of that long ago.

Some people called him an old soul. Maybe. He was only twenty-seven years old, but he'd always been years ahead of his friends and peers. The things they enjoyed were stuff he'd moved on from and had no intention of bringing back into his life.

He preferred to think of himself as a workaholic. While old friends or colleagues were out having a good time, partying, bouncing from bar to bar, he was at home building his empire. The plan was to retire when he was forty. So far, Imad was ahead of schedule, and this gem his contact with Interpol had given him would go a long way to helping him stay on track.

His eyes fixed on the three distinguished Flame Towers, a trio of imposing skyscrapers rising up over the backdrop of beige buildings and colorful apartment complexes. He twisted his head slightly and gazed at the architectural marvel known as SOCAR Tower with its bending, bulging upper section that seemed to defy gravity. The building was bathed in colorful lights and, with the Flame Towers, was easily one of the most recognizable buildings in all of Baku.

Imad let the curtain fall back into place and looked over his shoulder at the computer screens in the corner. The software was still running at an incredible pace, but the screens had already begun eliminating the potentials that didn't match all of the facial characteristics of the suspects.

He walked back over to the desk and eased into his chair as the application finished its job and began posting a series of photos.

In the new images, none of the men were together. The two guys who'd broken the old man out of the SUV in Liverpool were never in the same picture with the other. The old guy, too, was always on his own. Whoever they were, these men were no fools. Based on what the photo evidence was telling Imad, they were well aware of the surveillance nearly every airport on the planet deployed.

They weren't, however, careful enough to not be spotted eventually.

"I guess they didn't count on me."

The cat raised its head again, the eyes narrowly glaring at her owner, before lowering her chin back to the cushion and returning to a shallow slumber.

"Okay," Imad said to himself. "Let's find out where you three flew out of."

He already recognized one of the airport terminals. It was easy to spot since the writing on one of the walls behind the target was written in German. He also knew the color scheme in the decor.

"You flew out of Frankfurt, huh? That's interesting."

He took the image and dragged it over to the far-right screen and typed a quick tag on it so he could reference it later without a fuss.

Then he gazed at the next guy, the other young man in the group of three. The terminal he was walking through wasn't as readily identifiable, but that was fine. Imad could scratch Frankfurt off the list.

Sometimes, people who were trying not to be seen with one

another would still fly out of the same airport, simply separating themselves by time. These three suspects had been smarter than that, each taking different flights from different airports and likely keeping things even more covert by doing it at different times of day, possibly not even on the same day.

"You can't hide from me," Imad said with a clenched jaw.

He scoured the image and found a fragment of a word in the top-right corner. It was in a language he didn't immediately recognize. Then he pulled up a dozen airports in the surrounding area, comparing it with the largest first and then down to some of the midsize airports with fewer terminals. Imad pored over one, then another and another until he finally gave up and created a new search with different parameters.

He let out an exasperated sigh and ran his fingers through his hair again as the computer pulled up images that looked vaguely similar to the backdrop of the one with the second younger guy from the group of suspects. One of them was nearly identical.

Imad cocked his head to the right and scratched his neck, then analyzed the two images further.

"Yep, that's the one," he said after another minute. He moved the images over to the other screen, next to the first. "Bucharest. Gotcha."

"Now for you, old fellow."

Once more, he moved the mouse quickly back and forth, clicking at a rapid pace until he had things sorted the way he wanted them. Then Imad's fingers once more flew over the keys, typing in the search parameters.

"Let's see where you came from."

17

COPENHAGEN

The phone rang twice before June answered. She'd just stepped out of the shower only minutes before. Her shoulder-length brown hair was still wet, hanging over the white robe she wore. At times like these, taking five minutes to get a shower and wash her hair felt like a guilty pleasure.

Night had fallen over the city of Copenhagen. Adriana had decided that staying across the bridge in the Danish town would be a better idea, not necessarily to get away from the viral outbreak but because she was more familiar with it than the Swedish city.

She'd managed to find a room in a cozy little hotel not far from Nyhavn, one of her favorite areas of Copenhagen. It featured colorful buildings atop a seventeenth-century waterfront. Nyhavn was where Hans Christian Andersen had spent many days sitting at a table in front of his modest apartment, writing some of the most famous fairy tales of all time.

"I was just about to call you," June said. Her voice cracked and sounded like she'd been yelling at a football game all day. It was late in Copenhagen and Lyon was in the same time zone. Adriana figured her friend had been working tirelessly over the course of the day.

One truth always came to light during times like these. No matter how desperate the situation might be, a human body needed rest sooner or later. It was inevitable. Adriana could feel the bed in the next room calling to her.

"That means you have something to tell me."

"I do," June confirmed. Despite the fatigue, there was a twinge of hope in her voice. "Our contact in Azerbaijan has confirmed the identities of the two men who took our informant."

"Really?" Adriana blurted. "How'd he manage that? I figured Interpol would have the resources to handle that."

"They do, but I guess this guy is some kind of wizard with that sort of thing. He not only got their identities but everything else about them: where they're from, their last known residence, and most importantly, where they flew to from Baku."

"Outstanding. Where do I go?"

June hesitated, casting an awkward silence over the conversation.

"June?"

A sigh came through the device's earpiece. "Pavard sent his team in to handle it."

Another pause cut through the discussion.

"He took over your operation?" Adriana asked.

"I let him. I don't have enough people right now. We needed resources. Pavard offered. He has a good unit in place."

"Where are they?" Adriana remained on the point.

"Did you hear what I just said? Pavard's unit is going to run point on this. You and I are support."

Adriana knew June wouldn't give up pursuit that way if she didn't have a good reason. She'd given the biggest one. They didn't have anything anymore except a collection of agents and whatever weapons they'd been carrying at the time of the explosion. Getting armed wasn't an issue. It was all the other stuff: communications, planning and coordinating, clearing through government channels. Now that Shadow Cell was essentially a nomad organization, none of that stuff was quick or easy to come by. That would change in the coming months. June would rebuild, recoup, but for the moment things were challenging to say the least.

"I heard you," Adriana clarified.

June caught her friend's tone and understood. Adriana was a wild mustang. There was no keeping her hemmed in a coral. She ran free. One way or the other, Adriana would find out where Pavard's crew went.

"Uzbekistan," June relented. "Pavard's guy in Baku tracked their movement to Samarkand in Uzbekistan. Once we knew which city they went to and were able to tap into the surveillance footage there, pinpointing their exact location was easy. The Interpol office in Uzbekistan has been extremely good at helping track down the Teacher and his two henchmen."

"When are they going in?"

"First thing in the morning."

The gears turned in Adriana's mind. She could be there by morning if she found a flight. A quick glance at her watch narrowed that thin hope. Not at this hour. She doubted there were many flights heading to Samarkand. She'd need to find another way.

Luckily, there was a way she could have both.

"You're going to try to go to Samarkand, aren't you?" June's question cut the momentary silence.

"The Red Ring is much bigger and more powerful than we first suspected, June. I don't know if a unit from Interpol is ready for something like this."

She knew June was thinking the same thing. That's why Shadow Cell existed, to handle situations just like this one where the militaries of the world wouldn't step in and the police organizations like Interpol were ill equipped. Their officers were no slouches. They were well trained and some of the best on the planet. Still, that didn't mean they were ready for something of this magnitude.

"Not to mention I have a bad feeling about it," June added.

"You think it could be a trap?"

"I'd say anything is possible at this point." A couple of seconds passed before June spoke again. "Speaking of, what's happening in Malmö? I heard there's been some kind of turnaround with some of the victims."

Adriana cracked a smile. She hadn't heard. In fact, she'd been avoiding looking at news updates on her phone or the television because she didn't want to hear the death toll, knowing that little Johan's father would likely be one of the dead and assuming the mother didn't take action and give him the mixture she'd recommended.

"I hadn't heard."

"No?" June's interest was certainly piqued. "You were just there a few hours ago?"

Adriana glanced at the clock on the nightstand. It had been more than a few hours. She also knew the concoction she'd given the boy's mother was strong, but it didn't work that fast. It needed three to four hours to kick in, maybe five to start relieving the symptoms.

The healer had never given a specific range of effectiveness for the secret brew, only that it took a little time. Less than a day but more than a few minutes.

"It seems that one of the patients from the stadium is getting better. Sounds like he's in full recovery."

"Really? That's good news." Adriana played it off.

"And you know nothing about it?" June didn't buy it. There was no way it was a coincidence that Adriana was at the hospital several hours before and then people started miraculously getting better.

June didn't say anything for several seconds. "You wouldn't happen to know anything about that, would you?"

"No idea what you're talking about." She quickly moved the conversation along. "I did, however, find some interesting information from the cops."

"Yeah?" June ignored what she knew was a lie from her friend.

"I checked the security footage at the football stadium. We got a positive ID on the men who rigged the blimps."

"Really?"

"You sound so surprised. And here I thought you trusted me to get the job done."

June allowed a short laugh to burst through her lips. "Who are they?"

"The Swedes are tracking them down now. Last they saw, the men had crossed into Germany. They'll find them soon, I think. Maybe those two can shed some light on things for us. Although in light of what you told me before, maybe we don't need them."

"No," June corrected her. "Bring them in. You can never be too careful, and besides, the last thing we want is a couple of terrorists roaming the continent."

It was good point. "Unlike some of the others, these two do have known terrorist affiliations. They were working with another group out of Syria before bolting for the Red Ring. Apparently, these guys seem to be drawn to the next hottest thing in terrorist warfare."

"Keep me updated on what you learn from the Swedes. We need to make sure those two don't get away. Understood?"

"Got it. I'll take care of it, personally."

"Thank you." June waited for a couple of seconds before she continued. "And thank you for helping those people in Malmö. It looks like they're going to be okay. Whatever you did, I think it's going to save a lot of lives."

"No clue what you're talking about."

"Adriana, I saw the little boy on the news. He and his mother talked about a woman with a Spanish accent who came to the hospital and gave them a recipe for some kind of special tea. That tea is killing whatever flu is ravaging the area. I don't know where you got that brew or how you heard of it, but it's some kind of miracle drug."

"It's not a drug," Adriana said. "It's just something I learned about a long time ago when I was young. I met an old man who ran a spiritual hospital. He was a healer." She shook her head. "Look, we're wasting time. I need to get to Samarkand."

"By the time you get there, Pavard's team will have already done their thing. At that point, it will just be cleanup."

"You sound pretty sure about that." Adriana had a mountain of doubts and made no effort to hide it.

"What else can I do right now?"

Adriana had a few ideas. "I'm going to Samarkand. You can join me, or you can monitor from Lyon. Either way, I'm finding the first ticket to Uzbekistan, and I'm taking it."

June already knew her friend meant every word. There was nothing that could keep Adriana from doing something once her mind was set. She knew what Adriana really meant, too, when she made her comment about joining or staying in France. It was a lead, follow, or get out of the way kind of statement.

What could it hurt? She wasn't doing anything in Lyon at this point. Things were out of her hands. If she went to Uzbekistan, however, and something went wrong—heaven forbid—she could be close to lend a hand.

"Fine. Wait for me. I'll pick you up."

18

UZBEKISTAN COUNTRYSIDE

On the edge of the mountains in Uzbekistan, the Teacher looked out the window of his sitting room and gazed at the dramatic, sweeping vistas. A few of the higher peaks still showed signs of late spring, capped with faint traces of snow. Most of it was gone, but a select cluster of peaks seemed to hold on longer than the rest.

He picked up a cup of tea sitting on the table next to him and drew a long sip of the dark brew. It was his guilty pleasure—if there was anything guilty about it—and he indulged multiple times a day.

The Teacher heard the footsteps coming almost a full minute before Aziz turned the corner and appeared in the doorway. The old man didn't have to look to see who it was. That long gate, the staccato of the hard soles tapping on the tile floor, the determined tempo of the steps all signaled it was his second-in-command.

"What's the problem, Aziz?" the Teacher asked, still holding the cup in his hand and looking out the window.

The younger man stepped into the room, wearing a puzzled look on his face. "How did you know?"

"That it was you? Or that something was wrong?"

Aziz strode across the room and stopped next to the sofa, looking down at his master with shame in his eyes.

"Both."

"I'd recognize the sound of your footsteps anywhere, my old friend. You walk with purpose. I like that about you. Never wasting time, always pushing forward to make sure things get done. Today, however, you're walking a little faster, which means you have something urgent to tell me. From the look on your face, I can see it isn't good news."

"The people in Malmö..." Aziz didn't finish the thought right away.

"What about them?" The Teacher sat up a tad straighter.

"Something is wrong with the virus, sir. The people are getting better. It killed a handful early on, but now most of them are going into full recovery. Some of the news outlets are calling it...a miracle."

The Teacher set his cup down on a saucer with a loud clank. He stood and stormed over to the television on the wall at the far end of the long room. His robes flowed around him as he moved. He picked up a remote and turned on the television, switching it to one of the international news channels he received with his satellite dish.

They waited for a few minutes, through reports of economic upturn and weather catastrophes, before the woman on the screen finally looped around to the coverage of the Malmö Miracle.

That's what they were calling it. The headline glared at the Teacher in bold white letters on the top of the screen.

"What was looking like an outbreak of epic proportions is turning out to be not as bad as everyone first suspected," the woman said. *"Victims of the influenza epidemic that struck just a few short days ago are now having a remarkable turnaround, and it seems nearly everyone is going into full recovery thanks to a mysterious stranger."*

"Stranger?" The Teacher's eyes narrowed as he glared at the screen. "What does she mean?"

Aziz pointed at the screen and nodded, knowing what she was going to say next. He'd seen the story more than once and knew how the media worked. They cycled through the same story over and over again to make certain everyone saw it.

A young boy appeared on the screen standing next to a blonde woman both men figured to be his mother.

"She was an angel," the boy said. His name appeared at the bottom of the screen as Johan with the word *Witness* italicized. *"She saved my dad."*

The screen switched to a man sitting up in a bed. His blond hair was brushed to the side. A thick, reddish-blond beard covered his face. The guy was smiling as he tousled his son's hair.

"The stranger this boy and others are talking about," the news anchor returned to the screen, *"has not been located, but authorities are doing their best to find out just who this woman is and how she was able to come up with a treatment that hundreds of scientists and medical professionals couldn't."*

The screen switched to a doctor in a lab coat standing next to a reporter with a microphone. The physician wore gray glasses with flat temples reaching back to his ears and a black front. The man looked baffled, at one point even throwing up his hands as he spoke.

"We in the medical field realize that, from time to time, unexplainable things do occur. Sometimes, people call those things miracles. While many of us do not subscribe to things some would call miracles, it is certainly worth investigating, especially a situation such as this. I'm sure there's a scientific explanation and I, for one, would love to learn exactly what that explanation is."

"What kind of medicine did this woman give that boy for his father?"

The doctor blushed, his cheeks turning a bright red. He cleared his throat, clearly unwilling to give the answer for all the world to know.

"Well, um, it was a special kind of tea. To be honest, I'd never heard of it before, and some of the ingredients on the list she gave that boy aren't always easy to find. Luckily for them, there is a specialty store here in Malmö that sells everything they needed."

The reporter pressed the issue. *"Would you say maybe it's time to start investigating using something like this on other viruses or diseases?"*

The doctor chuckled. *"Well, while in this instance this natural remedy seems to be helping, there really is no replacement for good scientific research and study. We will be taking this strange brew in for more analysis to see exactly what makes it work and why it has been so effective against this particular strain of influenza; however we are confident this is an outlier and will continue to rely on modern medicine to treat the world's problems until it's been proved otherwise."*

The screen returned to the anchor. A sketch of a woman with dark hair appeared in the corner. The title *Angel of Malmö* loomed underneath it.

"Authorities continue to search for the so-called Angel of Malmö, but as yet have failed to locate her. This sketch was created with descriptions from young Johan and his mother. If you have seen this woman, authorities would appreciate any information you could give as to her whereabouts. I have a feeling they would like to thank her for her help. And so would Johan."

The anchor smiled and then started jabbering about something else going on in the world.

The Teacher's right eye twitched. He hit pause on the television and then backed it up thirty seconds to see the image in the top right once more. The letters spelling out *Angel of Malmö* glared at him. He clenched his jaw, immediately recognizing the woman.

The lines were simple sketches, rough and unrefined, but there was no mistaking her identity. It was the woman from Shadow Cell.

The Teacher had restrained his emotions, holding them in check as he stood in the room with her, watching their little operation destroy the dummy targets he'd so happily given them.

They, of course, had been clueless, thinking each installation possessed most of the Red Ring's arsenal. The agency bought the lie and was all too happy to take out the facilities, not realizing that most of their weapons and biological capabilities were safely tucked away in Uzbekistan, far from the targets being bombed.

"She should be dead," the Teacher stated, his voice full of disgust. "Why is she not dead?"

"We're not certain."

That wasn't good enough, and both men knew it.

Aziz felt ashamed, while his leader's emotions were bent toward rage. He'd witnessed everything during the escape. His men had perfectly executed the plan, cutting down the agents with extraordinary precision. It had been a dangerous proposition, having his men fire into the SUV with the Teacher sitting in the back, helpless. Their shots had been true, though, only taking down the targets in the front without any rounds punching through to the back.

Of course, he'd ducked down low two seconds before the firing began. His shooters knew to keep their shots high enough to not send a stray bullet into the back at a height that would hit the Teacher. They'd practiced everything for weeks, making sure their timing was perfect; their aims even more so.

When the Teacher exited the SUV, he knew the woman to his right wasn't hit, which was also why he'd ordered the explosive device be tossed under the vehicle's carriage. That should have cleared up any loose ends, taking Adriana Villa out of the picture. Yet here she was, swooping into Sweden to ruin his plans. If she'd found some kind of antidote for his virus, it wouldn't be long until the recipe spread throughout the world.

They needed to act fast before this so-called miracle got out of hand.

He shook his head. Things were coming unraveled. The Teacher could sense it. But he didn't understand. The men who extracted him from the SUV had thrown a powerful explosive under the vehicle. He'd seen it blow as they pulled away into the chaos. The sound, the fiery blast, all of it led to one clear conclusion. No one in the SUV would be left alive.

How had she survived that?

"I thought the men who got you out killed everyone in the car," Aziz said. He was simply trying to understand the same thing the Teacher wanted to figure out. The lieutenant wasn't trying to poke the bear, but he immediately got the sense that's exactly what he'd done. "I mean no disrespect, sir."

"I know you don't." The Teacher waved it off, but irritation dug at him like a splinter in his finger, nagging, constantly in the front of his mind. "She should be dead. I saw the car blow up. No one could survive that."

Yet she had. Had that been another miracle? Now she had stemmed the outbreak in Malmö, the very place he'd released a virus that should have been killing people by the tens of thousands. Except it wasn't. People were being cured with some kind of exotic tonic she'd concocted and given to a single patient.

"We need to hit the other targets, and quickly," the Teacher blurted. "Are the men in place?"

"Yes, Master, but what good will it do? The cure is out there now. All people will have to do is gather the items together, and the illness will go away."

"I don't need you tell me that, Aziz. Know your place."

Aziz swallowed and bowed his head, immediately ashamed of his insolence. "My apologies, Teacher. I simply wanted—"

"Unleash the virus on all the targets. Do it right away."

"All the targets?" Aziz still sounded unsure of the idea. They'd already changed plans once; now they were reverting back to something more like the original. Hitting all the targets now, however, would take an incredible amount of coordination and logistics. "Our men aren't positioned to hit all of them, sir." He feared the wrath he was certain to be inevitable.

The Teacher let out a haunting yell that echoed through the stone chamber and out into the day. He continued his roar as he threw the remote control against the wall, shattering it into several pieces. Buttons and bits of black plastic scattered onto the tile floor.

The old man breathed hard. A wheezing sound escaped his mouth, but Aziz said nothing. He would never suggest his leader might be sick or have some kind of health-related issue. He knew better. To do so would be to insinuate weakness, and no one did that —at least, no one did it and survived.

Once he'd calmed down a bit, the Teacher considered the problem. "How many are in position and ready to strike?"

"At last check? Six. We can probably have two more in place

within an hour. Some of the others will take a day or two. Most can be ready by nightfall."

"So, perhaps ten targets could be hit by the time the sun sets tonight."

"Yes, sir. Possibly more." Aziz knew that it was the Teacher's own fault things were going to be delayed. It was, after all, the old man who had ordered a change of plans, a direction that would make things seem like a natural outbreak of the virus. All that was gone now. Aziz was fine with that. He came from the old-school mindset that when you struck at the heart of an infidel, you let the world know about it. This running and hiding behind a virus wasn't the way he wanted to do things. If the Teacher ordered him to walk into a school with a bomb strapped to his chest, he would do it in a heartbeat.

That, however, wasn't the way his leader did things. Aziz wasn't so foolish or shortsighted to think his way was better. This man had brought about a brilliant strategy and one that had frustrated the West for a long time. His leadership was cunning and unlike any Aziz had ever seen before. The mere fact that the Teacher had gone into the proverbial belly of the beast and taken down a covert agency in the UK was enough for him to serve the Teacher until the end of his days. That didn't mean now and then he didn't disagree with certain decisions.

There was no point in lamenting the past. What was done was unchangeable. They could only move forward.

"Hit them all, all of them you can, at least. If they have a remedy for what we have created, it will take time to manufacture it to the level they'll need to save everyone. At the very least, we can weaken the world's populations. When we do, taking down their infrastructure will be easier. We will send them back to the Dark Ages."

"I'll alert the men, sir. All will be done as you direct."

19

SAMARKAND, UZBEKISTAN

Adriana and June watched the monitor with a gaze as intense as the Uzbekistani sun. The laptop was set up on a metal folding table the Interpol team had brought with them. Gear bags and crates circled the table in a U shape within the confines of an abandoned building.

From the looks of it, the place had been a textile factory during Samarkand's heyday as a center for cotton and textile production. Faint traces of thread and fabric littered the floor around them. In the center of the big facility, two machines sat collecting dust. Each one displayed wheels, gears, and metal rods going through the center. Spindles were attached on the sides, though their threads were long gone. The rest of the machines must have been removed during the final days of factory operation. Strange that two of the looms, or whatever they were, still remained.

Adriana had seen that sort of thing before when businesses shut down. Often, they collected the essentials and then left as quickly as possible. She wasn't entirely sure why that was the case.

Whatever the reason, it gave her and the rest of the Interpol team the perfect place to stage their operation.

The two women were outsiders despite Pavard giving them

authority to be there. Because of that, the group from the local Interpol branch was running things on their own, while Adriana and June were resigned to watching from the temporary HQ.

They understood, of course. June wouldn't have wanted a couple of strangers thrust into their midst while a mission like this was being thrown together. The Samarkand Interpol group was a good one, and she knew that. They'd handle their business like pros, although she knew no one on their team was as good as Adriana. She was the best June had seen, which was why she was there.

June knew, though, that Adriana wasn't long for this gig. She'd been reluctant to come in, only being pushed into it because of a terrorist attack she'd seen with her own eyes. There was no doubt in June's mind, however, that Adriana was only going to be doing this on a part-time basis.

She knew Adriana needed to see Sean. The thought pushed a sting into her heart like a needle. She missed Tommy. Perhaps when this was over, when the Red Ring was put down for good and their despicable leader was either in custody or dead—she preferred the latter—they would be able to spend some time together.

On the monitor, the cops from Interpol surrounded the building. Normally, they wouldn't conduct a raid like this until after dark. Doing it at sunset would have to work. They'd already lost precious time getting this operation planned and organized. Luckily, Interpol had placed a person outside the building once they'd learned what was going on there. It had been under constant observation for the entire day. No one had left, which was strange—at least to June and Adriana—but the observer detected movement inside, which meant their targets were still there.

The target building didn't have many windows, and the ones it did have were shut so no one could see in or out. Interpol had used sensors to detect heat signatures inside. There weren't as many people as they might have thought, but there were still a few dozen or so. Throughout the day, as the team rendezvoused at the staging site, they kept a close watch on the men inside the building two blocks away on the other side of the street.

From the looks of it, the place was an old warehouse for produce, though that was just a guess. Abandoned buildings occupied a significant section of this part of town, the businesses either shutting down or moving their operations to a more profitable or convenient location in the world.

Samarkand was a fascinating place, boasting an interesting mix of ancient cultures, a struggle to revive them, and the continuous encroachment of the modern world.

The older parts of the city were some of the most well preserved historical locations in the region, if not the world. The Registan, the old name for the heart of the city, was still as beautiful as it must have been at the height of the medieval Timurid Dynasty. The majestic turquoise dome stood offset against the three surrounding majolica-covered madrassas as well as the Gūr-e-Amīr, the spectacular tomb of Timur, known to most lay historians as the great conqueror Tamerlane.

Then there were the slums where much of the population struggled to make it. The buildings were rundown; some probably would have been condemned long ago if it weren't for the occupation of derelict citizenry.

Last was the downtown area where tall skyscrapers rose above the desert floor and stood against the backdrop of the mountains in the distance, challenging them for supremacy over the city. Some businesses and commerce, Adriana knew, could thrive anywhere.

In its heyday, the city of Samarkand was in a prime location along the fabled Silk Road connecting Asia to the Mediterranean and the West. The city grew as a result of the constant trade between the regions, and the population swelled over the centuries.

In recent history, the nation was swallowed up by the Soviet Union until 1991 and the collapse of the communist regime. Remarkably, much of the culture remained intact. Uzbekistan was far enough from Moscow that the far-reaching arm of the Soviets seemed content that it was simply part of the nation. The Russians had also been so preoccupied with expansion and the Cold War with the United States that exacting much of the control they'd been able to enforce in regions closer to Moscow was neither practical nor effective this far away.

Stalin had done his best to remove nationalist supporters from the government, executing many of them and sending others into exile. The leaders that followed had developed a laxer approach to the region, and as a result the city of Samarkand and the nation as a whole slipped back into their old traditions and cultural norms without much pressure from Moscow.

During World War II, Stalin had relocated many factories and weapons production facilities to the area. Adriana wondered if the building they were in and the one they were observing on the computer screen were two such buildings. She twisted her head around and inspected the architecture and design for the first time since arriving. She'd been so intent on making sure the mission went smoothly and paying attention to everything that was going on, she'd not even really noticed the interior of the place. Upon quick examination, Adriana was certain these structures dated back to the early 1940s.

On the screen, one of the operatives moved toward the rear door. The plan was to go in from the back, cutting off any rear-retreat by the terrorists. Then if they tried to go out the front, another complement of Interpol agents would push in through the entrance and hem them in.

The plan was solid, though Adriana and June both had doubts. It couldn't be that simple, could it? Their concern over the ease of the operation may have just been old-fashioned paranoia, something both of them suffered with seemingly increasing frequency.

That was something Adriana and Sean certainly had in common. A healthy dose of fear with a pinch of suspicion had kept them alive more times than she could count. June came from the same ilk, always alert and ready for almost anything.

Lights flickered on outside the building as the sun continued to set, casting shadows over the building and those surrounding it. The street grew darker by the second along with the open corridors that ran along the external walls of the old factory.

The guy running the show stood closest to the table in the staging area. He was average height, around five feet and eight inches. He had jet-black hair, matching thick eyebrows, and a light tan that so many of the people in the region sported.

Elman Hamidov had been kind enough to let the two rogue agents—at least, that's how he viewed them—participate by being there, but he was clear that they could not interfere with the actual takedown of these terrorists.

June understood. She ran a tight ship, too, and had no intention of getting in the way of someone else's operation, even though it had been her agency that put everything in play and had been chasing the Red Ring for well over a year.

That didn't matter. June was willing to put her ego aside to make sure these men paid for what they'd done, not only to her agency and two of its operatives, but to innocent people all over the world. She wanted them to be an example that terrorism would never prevail and would always meet a gruesome end.

"Go," Elman said into his radio.

He watched the screen like a symphony conductor eyeing every musician in the chamber, exacting ultimate control and precision.

One of the cops was carrying a tactical battering ram. He stepped around the two closest to the entrance of the building and swung his arms back in a wide arch. When the heavy object reached its zenith, he twisted his torso back around, letting the big muscles of his body do most of the work.

The black piece of steel pounded the metal door and burst it open in one powerful strike. The frame around the latch sparked and bent out of shape from the brute-force entry.

Then, in an instant, the Interpol team flooded the building.

Elman turned his head to the second screen on the right as the unit positioned at the rear of the building charged through the back door. Initially, the screen to the right was dark, but the agent with the camera switched on their night-vision goggles and suddenly the screen was bathed in a greenish-white glow.

Pillars of steel rose to the ceiling around the officers as they split up, each taking cover behind the columns. Some took positions next to old wooden crates stacked long the wall. A door at the other end led into the main portion of the building where Elman knew team one was already pushing through.

He turned his attention back to the first screen and watched as the unit poured into the area. He squinted at the scene playing out in front of him. The expectation was that they'd find a few dozen terrorists inside working furiously to pack and transport weapons, explosives, and other contraband.

What Elman was seeing on the screen wasn't at all what he'd expected.

The people inside were moving around in seemingly random directions. All had hoods over their heads to prevent them from seeing where they were going. They were, essentially, walking like zombies around the huge room with their hands bound behind their backs.

"What in the world?"

Alarms went off in Adriana's head. She glanced across her shoulder at June and instantly saw that she had the exact same concern.

"Elman," June said, urgency filling her voice, "get your people out of there now."

He turned toward her with an angry glare. "We agreed this was my operation. My team, my people, my operation. I thought you weren't going to interfere."

"It's a trap, Elman. You need to get them out. Now." June's tone carried the authority she didn't, but that wouldn't change the man's mind. She'd determined how headstrong he was upon meeting him for the first time.

"Keep quiet, or I will have you escorted out of here."

He kept his eyes locked on the screens, looking from one to the other. One of the officers moved closer to a person with a hood over their head. The hands were old, tanned, worn. They looked like they belonged to a person who'd been working outdoors their entire life, perhaps on a farm. The skin on the wrists was the same, wrinkled and weathered.

The agent stopped close to the old man and grabbed him from behind and pulled him backward toward one of the big crates near the entrance.

"These people are all prisoners," Elman said. "Get the rest of them out of there, then search the building for the terrorists responsible."

June shook her head. She wanted to punch the man in the back of the head and take his radio from him, but that wouldn't fly. There were two other Interpol cops standing in the room on either side of her and Adriana. A move like that would receive similar treatment from them, along with criminal charges and time spent in an Uzbekistani jail.

She bit her tongue and watched, hoping she was wrong.

The door at the other end of the building burst open, and the team coming in from the other side flooded the floor space, spreading out to cover every angle and every potential shooting spot where an enemy could have been waiting in ambush.

The agents who'd come in from the front continued to split up. Some stayed back behind crates, keeping their weapons moving back and forth, sweeping the massive space, ready to take out a target should they show themselves.

"Sir, there are no targets. Only prisoners."

The voice came through the radio on the table as well as on Elman's personal one. Adriana scowled for a moment, and then her eyes widened. "Oh no."

The words had barely passed through her lips when the screens filled with a bright white flash. Then they went black as the building shook around them all the way down to the foundation.

The light fixtures on the wall and those hanging from the ceiling far above rattled and swung back and forth. The table trembled violently, and one of the screens fell over onto its back.

"Team one," Elman said into his radio. "What was that?"

No answer.

The lights flickered back on around them, and the shaking stopped.

"Team one, do you copy? Come in, team one."

Still nothing.

"Team two, do you copy? Come in, team two."

He received no answer. The young woman working the communications system at the table turned and looked back up at him. She shook her head, letting him know there was no signal coming in from the other units.

Elman stared at the blank screens, blinking rapidly in disbelief. He put his hand over his mouth, dragged it across his lips, lengthening his face for a second and causing the skin below his eyes to sag.

He stormed away from the table toward the door and pushed through it. The two cops standing behind the Shadow Cell agents took off after him and followed the man outside.

Adriana and June glanced at each other with the same question showing in their eyes. Their hearts ached because they already knew what happened in the building a few blocks away.

They turned and followed the remnants of the Interpol team outside and down the sidewalk. It only took a second for them to see what happened with their own eyes. Elman staggered for a moment and then sped up to a full sprint, charging across the empty street.

Just beyond the worn-down factories and warehouses, a pillar of black smoke tumbled into the darkening evening sky. At the base, dark orange flames roiled upward, the fire consuming the building in a furious blaze.

When the group rounded the last corner, their fears soured into a bitter reality. The entire facility was consumed in searing flames.

No one inside could have survived.

20

UZBEKISTAN COUNTRYSIDE

The Teacher looked out his window toward the city of Samarkand in the distance. He was far enough away that neither he nor anyone in his palace felt the ground tremble at the explosion. He couldn't even make out the smoke from the fire over the skyline. Had it been daytime, the black clouds pouring out of the destroyed facility would have been visible from hundreds of miles away.

He'd received the tip from one of his sources within the local Interpol office. His connection was a new cop, recently hired to the unit. What his superiors didn't know was that the young man was working for the Red Ring and infiltrating their department to keep tabs on things just in case someone ever came close to tracking down the Teacher and his followers.

Six months on the job, and nothing had happened.

Then, out of nowhere, the mole learned of a raid in the early morning hours. The local Interpol branch had been alerted that he and his two associates had traveled to Samarkand as the last stop on their journey from Liverpool.

How had this happened? The Teacher wasn't sure, but then again he wasn't sure how the woman had survived the blast in England, either. More and more of the unexplainable was starting to happen, and if he was a less patient person, given easily to panic, he might have tried to flee the country.

The Teacher, however, always had a backup plan. The minute he learned of the Interpol investigation, he had his men evacuate the building, making sure to take everything of importance they could before leaving behind a few dozen slaves they'd been using for grunt work during the course of operations.

Slaves were easy to come by and relatively inexpensive when one knew where to look. And the Teacher had connections in some of the seediest places.

He had no moral problem with buying slaves, using them for labor, and then making them a sacrifice. They were, after all, nothing more than tools for the plans of almighty Allah to cleanse the earth.

The slaves were bound and hooded to keep them from escaping. Then they were left there as a distraction for the imminent attack by Interpol. The building had been rigged with enough ordnance to wipe out half a city block and easily destroy the entire structure along with everything and everyone inside.

A phone on the nearby counter rang. The Teacher stepped away from the window and picked it up. He didn't have to look at the screen to know it was Aziz. Only he and one other person had that particular number, the other being the mole.

"Is it taken care of?" The Teacher didn't have to ask, not normally. But things were suddenly starting to unravel. It wasn't that the old man was unaccustomed to challenges. Trials were part of life. They made you what you were. This, however, was different.

He'd planned everything to the last detail. Hadn't he? The doubt in his mind vanished as the Aziz's voice came through the phone.

"Yes, Teacher. The problem has been taken care of."

The words filled the Teacher's ear and flooded him with relief. Finally, something went the way it was supposed to.

"Thank you. Return to me. We have preparations to make."

"I'm walking into the building now."

The Teacher ended the call. He appreciated that kind of efficiency from Aziz. The old man would say jump, and Aziz would ask how high on the way up. It was one of the reasons the Teacher trusted the younger man as much as he did, with as much as he did. Aziz was now running most of the operations, coordinating more than the Teacher ever had.

The old man was glad for that. He didn't care for handling all the details. That was a young man's game. He wanted to simply do the planning, give inspiration to those who needed it, and be a spiritual guide to lost sheep all over the world.

He shuffled over to the window and gazed out into the desert night sky. Billions of stars twinkled bright against a black blanket. A crescent moon was shining over the city in the distance. The Teacher drew in a long breath of the dry air and exhaled with a short prayer of gratitude for the moment. He was doing the work of the Almighty and considered the task a tremendous honor.

He had, of course, benefited from all his work. This palace wasn't cheap. Neither were the luxurious cars in his garage. He had, after all, front-loaded his life sacrifices many years ago. There was nothing wrong with having a few nice things. At least that's how he justified it. Besides, luxury conveyed power. He had to qualify it to his men as a way that Allah was taking care of him while they mostly slept in small dorms or cells across the country and in various locations around the Middle East.

The Teacher thought about his teams around the world unleashing their virus into society. He'd seen the news reports. Some of the men had been caught. Most hadn't.

The attacks had rendered the desired effect, at least in the beginning, but one by one, each city followed the same treatment procedure as Malmö as word spread almost instantly about a special tea that could cure the illness.

Most of the major targets were already treating the virus with tremendous success, though there were some areas that had trouble getting the volume of the concoction they needed to treat everyone.

There had been some deaths as a result, but not nearly to the level the Teacher had hoped.

He wasn't in a good mood when Aziz walked in the room, his breath coming quickly from hurrying up the stairs and down the long corridors.

At least they'd eliminated the task force from Interpol. Their resources would be significantly depleted for the immediate future. He hoped that the entire organization would take the hint and back off from any further investigation, but the old man knew that effect wouldn't last long.

Sooner or later, they would come after him again. Time was running out, and the original plan's viability was falling through the bottleneck of the hourglass at breakneck speed.

There was only one thing to do now.

"Thank you for coming so quickly, my old friend." The Teacher bowed his head to Aziz, who returned the gesture by lowering his head farther than his master. It was a sign of respect for the man who had taken him from nothing and given him a purpose, a sense of reason in a chaotic world.

"I came as quickly as I could, sir."

The old man knew he had and nodded in acknowledgment. Then he coughed hard, hit with a spasm that racked his body for fifteen seconds. He covered his mouth for a moment and then wiped his lips, hoping Aziz didn't notice the thin crimson liquid streaking across his hand.

"Master? Are you all right?"

The Teacher dismissed the question with his right hand. "We... must accelerate our plans once more, Aziz." His voice came in a crackled rasp.

"Sir, you need to rest. Please, come over here and sit down." He motioned to the sofa nearby.

"No, my Son. You must not worry about me. I'll be fine. We are close now."

"Master, the virus is no longer working. The cure...they are treating anyone who gets sick with this strange mixture."

"Yes." The Teacher nodded and waved his hand in the air again. "I'm well aware of what is happening. I also know some of our men have been killed. The dark forces, it seems, are mounting against our holy cause."

Aziz's head bobbed up and down in agreement.

"We must go ahead with the second phase of the plan."

The look on Aziz's face changed. He cocked his head to the side, the brows over his eyes nearly touching from the scowl. "Sir? The infidels are not significantly weakened. Our plan was to kill them by the millions and then send our soldiers into the cities to exterminate the ones who remained."

"Plans, it seems, have to change, my dear Aziz." Before his lieutenant could speak up again in protest, the Teacher continued. "I realize that, for many, this will now be a suicide mission. Every man knew that could be the case when they joined our movement. Even you."

Aziz knew that to be the case and even then would gladly have given his life for their righteous cause.

"When will we launch the attack?" Aziz's question was direct, leaving no doubt in the mind of his leader that he would make certain everything was executed as directed.

"When the sun rises, thirty-six hours from now. I would prefer to strike at dawn tomorrow, but I realize our men need time to prepare, both spiritually and physically. As you said, many of them will die. They need to prepare their souls for paradise. When the sun rises here over this land, send out the message to all of them to attack. We will show the rest of the world that our resolve is strong, our mission is just, and from that, many more will flock to our movement."

It wasn't what the Teacher had wanted. Aziz knew it, too. The plan had been to cleanse the planet of the scourge humanity had transformed into. Now, things had changed. He and the Teacher would have to be satisfied with knowing they'd taken out as many infidels as possible. He knew his men were well armed and equipped to deal significant damage.

They might not have been able to kill the billions they'd hoped for, but even if they took out a few hundred thousand, that would be a start. Perhaps, if he lived long enough, the Teacher could devise a new plan, one that couldn't be stopped.

He cringed. The burning in his lungs sent him the depressing message loud and clear. He wasn't going to have that kind of time. The woman from the picture on the news, the one he'd been in the car with in England, had ruined everything. How could one person, especially an insignificant creature like a woman, take down everything he'd worked and planned so hard to create, and in such a small amount of time?

He lamented the fact that she wasn't dead. If he'd been armed at the time, he would have done the deed himself, putting a bullet through one side of her skull and out the other.

There was no changing the past, so wishing it could be different was a fruitless endeavor.

He had to stay focused on what they could do now, which was hit the wicked of the world as fast and hard as they could.

Aziz knew what to do. They'd discussed this contingency plan before in case someone happened to wreck the original. He would send out a text message to the leaders of every individual cell positioned around the world. Once that message was sent, the men would emerge from their hiding places and unleash an attack on civilian targets unlike anything the world had ever seen before.

They were equipped with a wide array of guns, explosives, and other weapons that could deal out significant casualties to a civilian population. The men had also been trained to take on any military or police threats. They'd studied the tactics used by those kinds of enemies and would fight the good fight until the very last. Their goal was to hit highly populated areas in more than a dozen countries, taking out as many people as possible.

It wasn't the plan the Teacher wanted to use. This was a consolation prize. If he couldn't wipe the earth clean of the nonbelievers, he would—at the very least—make them live in fear for the rest of their lives. Not to mention the pain he would inflict on thousands of families. Perhaps then they would understand the power of the Red Ring and the god they served. It was the least he could do.

"Do it," the Teacher said.

Aziz nodded and walked out the door. He had his orders and knew all his brethren would follow theirs.

21

SAMARKAND

Elman didn't crack.

Adriana and June thought for sure the man would break down any second and start sobbing like a child as he stood outside the yellow police lines that stretched around the rubble.

The explosion had destroyed almost the entire building, leaving only the east wall standing—though it looked like it might collapse with even the slightest hint of wind. The only show of emotion the man allowed to display on his face came from the repeated clenching of his jaw as he watched the rescue teams and engineers attempt to remove debris from the site in hopes of finding survivors.

He knew better. He had to. Adriana and June had already resigned themselves that every Interpol agent that had gone into the building had died in the explosion or, at worst, from the structure collapsing down on them. Truth be told, everyone had likely died in an instant. The fire from the blast was too hot for any human to survive. The brick and mortar from the walls were charred black. Steel girders and beams had been softened to the point of bending in a few places.

The smoldering remains bore a grisly tribute to the power the

Red Ring possessed and the fact that they were more than willing to sacrifice lives to further their cause.

Elman spun around and eyed the two women with a venomous glare. "How did you know it was a trap?" He raised an accusing finger.

June frowned, glanced at Adriana, then back to him. "We tried to warn you, Elman. Don't even think about trying to put this on us. You should have seen it the second your team went in there. Those people inside were put there to make it look like the terrorists were doing business as usual, which means they knew the kind of surveillance tech you'd be using and the exact times you'd be preparing to go in."

He frowned the second he realized what she was insinuating. "What are you saying?"

"You know darn well what I'm saying, Elman. You have a mole in your outfit. Someone on the inside is working for the Teacher, and that person just cost you the lives of a lot of good agents."

He tossed his head to the side, throwing off the accusation. "I don't think you understand the gravity of what you're saying." He spat the words in a thick accent. Despite being from a foreign land, he had a strong grasp on the English language, even a bit of vocabulary that hinted at an approaching fluency.

Adriana stepped forward between the two of them. "With all due respect, sir, she understands exactly what she's saying. And I have to concur. There is no way these terrorists would have known what was coming unless they had a person on the inside. Someone in your organization tipped them off. It's the only explanation. Look at the facts. They knew when to blow the building. They placed human beings inside to make it appear they were still in there transporting something. And whoever detonated the explosives waited until the perfect moment when all your units were well inside the building. This was an inside job whether you want to admit it or not. I know that hurts to hear someone you trust has betrayed you, but if you refuse to take a look at that possibility, you won't ever figure out how this happened."

His jaw clenching continued, but Adriana saw that she'd struck a chord. He knew they were right, and he couldn't ignore it. Besides, he didn't get to be where he was in the agency without knowing what good police work was. Leaving no stone unturned was the key to any successful investigation.

He gave a nod. "You're right," he relented, lowering his voice to a whisper. "I don't like to admit it. No one in charge of any organization wants to confess to the possibility of a leak or a mole being anywhere close to them. But you're correct. I have to take a step back from my personal feelings and conduct a thorough investigation. I lost good people here today." He glanced over his shoulder, and when he turned back to face them tears welled in his eyes. "I will find whoever did this and make them pay. I promise you that."

"We will do whatever we can to help," June offered. Her voice had lost its edge, and now she sounded sympathetic, caring, like she did when she spoke to Tommy.

"Thank you." He twisted his head and wiped the back of his wrist across his eyes. "Now, if you'll excuse me, I need to facilitate this... effort." He held out a hand toward the mess. Cops were everywhere along with firefighters, EMTs, and other rescue crews.

"We understand," Adriana said. "Let us know if you need anything."

"I will."

The two women watched as Elman walked away, disappearing into a cloud of steam wafting off the debris.

"Let's get back to the staging area and collect our things," June said when he was out of earshot. "This thing is far from over, and we need to figure out how the Red Ring found out we were here and what we were doing."

Adriana's eyebrows lowered as she frowned. "Didn't he just say that he's going to work on it?"

"They have red tape to go through. You and I don't. Besides, his main objective is finding the mole, not the Red Ring. He could be wrapped up in that for weeks. We need to find this Teacher and his disciples and shut them down before they can kill anyone else."

The phone in her pocket started ringing. June let out a groan and fished the device out of her pants. "It's Pavard," she said with a glance at the screen.

The two continued walking toward the building where the temporary staging area was set up.

"This is June. Got anything for me, Olivier?"

"Unfortunately, yes."

"I don't like the sound of that."

"Well, it's not all bad news. Several more cities were hit by this flu outbreak. Turns out you were correct; it was definitely a terrorist attack."

"So, you figured that out?"

"Two of them were caught in Amsterdam trying to poison the water supply. They, apparently, committed suicide before they were able to be brought in for questioning. Another two were nearly captured in Hong Kong, but they engaged officers and were shot dead."

That was bad news. Had they been able to capture any of the attackers, the authorities might have been able to get information that could lead to the Teacher. Dead men weren't helpful in that regard.

"Got any good news for me?"

"Actually, yes. The virus has been neutralized for the most part. The antidote is being administered in every major city where this strain of influenza has popped up. So far, casualties have been kept to a minimum."

"Glad to hear it."

"I heard about the bombing in Samarkand. I was happy to hear the two of you are okay."

"Word travels fast," June quipped.

"In our world it does. Any idea what happened?"

June looked back over her shoulder at the destruction. "We think Elman had a mole in his unit. It's the only way all of this could have gone down. They were ambushed. The Red Ring knew we were here. They knew exactly when we'd hit the facility."

Pavard remained silent for several seconds before responding. "That's a serious insinuation."

"I know."

"Did you tell him?"

"Yeah."

"I guess he didn't take that well. I know I wouldn't have."

"No, and neither would I. Still, you have to look at every angle with these things. I'm willing to wager there aren't many weapons or munitions in that building. We won't know until things cool down and the investigators can really start digging through the debris, but yeah, I'd say they won't find a thing."

Adriana noted a white transport van parked at the other end of an alley as they passed by. There was an image of a bird on it surrounded by a circle.

They kept walking and turned into the building where the staging area was located.

"We're going to work on that," June said. "Elman will be tied up for a while with this whole mess. We don't have time to spare. We have to find the Teacher and bring this to an end. Otherwise, a lot more people are going to get hurt."

"Agreed." There was a resignation in Pavard's voice. "I'm sorry I couldn't be more help."

"You're doing more than anyone else could have, Olivier. Thank you."

"You're very welcome."

She ended the call as they neared a table where the two screens sat on the surface surrounded by wires, keyboards, and stacks of equipment. Cords ran out from the table into several metal crates containing communications and surveillance gear.

Adriana squinted hard. Curiosity crawled along her spine as they approached. A phone was sitting on the table next to a keyboard. "Is that Elman's?" she asked and twisted her head, stopping next to the table.

"Looks like the phone he was using earlier," June answered. "He must have left it here. We all kind of rushed out."

The device vibrated once, and the preview of a text message appeared on the screen.

"Strange," Adriana commented. She leaned closer. "Well done. Now eliminate the two women." The realization smacked them across the face. A sickening lump dropped from their throats, free falling into their stomachs. "Elman is the mole?"

She didn't know if she saw the hint of shadow wash over the far wall, or if it was some kind of sixth sense that picked up on the subtle movement, but Adriana instantly felt trouble.

"Get down!" She shoved June to the side, swiped the phone, and dove in the other direction as a gun fired from the doorway. Her movements were deft and all done in the span of less than two seconds.

Bullets ricocheted off the brick walls and concrete floors as Adriana rolled behind one of the crates near the table. June slid behind a stack of boxes. They wouldn't keep her safe from the gunfire, but being out of sight was a start.

"You know," Elman said, his voice bouncing off the walls amid a thin veil of gun smoke, "I really wanted to do this when you were in your hotel room." His heels clicked on the floor, a signal he was on the move but in a methodical, deliberate way. "You know, come in and shoot you both in the head while you slept. Something like that. What are you doing in here, June? Huh?"

Adriana clutched a pistol in one hand and the phone in the other, gently pressing her back against the crate so the stack didn't topple over. She swiped the screen with her thumb and saw that the device was locked, asking for facial recognition from the owner. When it didn't recognize her, it requested the lock code, which she didn't have. Yet.

"What did they pay you, Elman?" June shouted. "I hope it was a lot to sell your soul."

"You have no vision. Typical American. The Teacher offers more than just money. He offers a path to truth and righteousness."

"Cut the crap, Elman. He paid you."

A short chuckle resonated off the walls. "Of course he paid me. I'll never have to work a day in this stupid job again, ever."

"They kill innocent people, Elman. They're terrorists. That makes you a terrorist."

"Perhaps." The way he said it told Adriana he was moving again, like his head had twisted to the side or like he was getting farther away for a moment.

If he was on the move, he kept his steps silent, apparently aware of how loud they were on the hard floor.

Then the door abruptly closed, and a sound of metal on metal told the women he was locking it.

"There," Elman said. "That's better. We wouldn't want someone interfering with our little game."

Adriana sprang from her hiding place and fired a shot at him. He ducked down with a finger on the light switch by the door and flicked it off.

The room descended into pitch-black darkness, only illuminated for a moment by the residual glow from the gases within the bulbs overhead.

"Now we have a fun little game. I'd say the odds are more even now since there are two of you and one of me. Can't have the two of you trying to gang up."

Adriana cursed herself for missing the shot, but she'd had to take it quickly. Her ears rang a little from the discharge, but that was a part of this sort of thing she'd gotten over long ago.

"Why don't you just give yourself up, Elman?" June said. "This isn't going to end well for you."

The man laughed. As he bellowed, Adriana skirted out away from the crates and crouched next to the wall. If the man was equipped with night vision, he would have already fired. He was gambling, hoping he could level the field against the two women by playing in the dark. Then, at least, maybe he could get the drop on them.

Adriana saw through the ploy and immediately knew what June was doing by talking to him. She was trying to give away her position and isolate his. Maybe Elman realized it; maybe he didn't. From the duration of his laughter, evidently he didn't. Or perhaps he was playing his own game, trying to lure the women out of hiding so he could flip on the lights again and take them down.

From the sound of his voice, he was no longer moving.

Adriana slipped along the wall, careful to move her feet slowly in case there was something on the floor. The last thing she needed was to trip and make a bunch of noise.

She slowed her pace to a crawl, feeling as if she was getting close to the door where Elman had been standing.

"It doesn't have to be this way, Elman," June said. "You can take the easy way out and let us kill you, or you can come in and give us everything you know on the Red Ring."

The man laughed again. He was still right where he'd been before. His ruse was clear now. He was trying to lure them out so he could flash the lights on and take them by surprise. It wasn't the best plan, at least in Adriana's opinion, but she wasn't about to complain.

"You don't know much about them, do you?" Elman asked. "They are everywhere, June. They have unlimited reach and more money than you could ever imagine. No one double-crosses the Red Ring. No one."

Adriana could almost feel the man's panicky breath in the lingering bitter scent of burned gunpowder. Only a few feet away now. She said a silent prayer that he wouldn't turn the light on, putting her in an awkward position with no cover to be found.

"If you think you can get me to tell you anything about them, you're dead wrong, June. You and your friend are going to die here. I already called them. They will be here soon and have this entire building surrounded."

Adriana knew he was bluffing. The idiot had left his phone on the table.

She had no intention of bringing that up. She lowered down to the floor and shimmied forward and to the left, listening as she moved like a deadly snake across the concrete.

She could still hear his breathing. His feet shuffled to her right. He was so close now. Once she was behind him, close to the wall, she silently pushed herself up and took a step toward where she believed the man was standing.

"You're bluffing!" June shouted.

"Am I?"

Adriana pressed the muzzle of her pistol to the back of his skull. "Yes. You are."

22

SAMARKAND

Elman screamed at the top of his lungs. His desperate pleas and cries for mercy would go unheard. He was surrounded by two feet of concrete and steel in the warehouse's basement. Above, the additional layer of concrete would also keep his yelling muted to the outside world. No one, not even the remaining members of his team, would hear a thing.

He was bound to a chair with a healthy dose of duct tape the two women had found in the gear crates next to the staging area. The chair was a happy bonus, left there by the woman controlling the screens during the operation.

Adriana had gotten the drop on him, forced the weapon out of his hand so he couldn't kill himself, and then marched him down into the facility's basement.

The room contained an old boiler that looked like it hadn't been used in a century. Chains hung from the ceiling along the walls in a few spots. Dim fluorescent lights flickered in the center of the room, casting a sterile and eerily pale glow throughout the room.

Adriana stood in front of the prisoner, gripping the pistol barrel with one hand. She dangled it a few inches in front of Elman's groin, letting the grip swing back and forth like a pendulum. His legs were bound at the ankles but separated at the knees with a block of wood June found on the floor near the boiler.

"You don't understand!" Elman shouted. "They'll kill me!"

"We will kill you." June's statement didn't even contain the faintest hint of a lie.

"You don't have the—"

Adriana let the weapon swing forward a little faster, and the base of the grip struck him right where it hurt the most. It wasn't a bludgeoning strike or one that was driven home with a ton of force, but it didn't need to be.

He yelled out again as the nauseating pain coursed through his body, resonating out from the single point that felt like a hammer blow. The women had heard some of the foulest language known to mankind, but even they were taken aback by some of the creative profanities that flowed from the man's lips. Spittle shot across his lap with every word, emphasizing his unadulterated rage.

"Look, Elman," June said in a calming tone, "I don't want to keep hurting you. And I don't want Adriana to keep hurting you, but you're not giving us a ton of options here."

His groaning died down. His eyes bulged out of their sockets as he strained against the bonds that wouldn't break under the muscles of a man twice his size.

"And before you tell us something offensive or where we can go, keep in mind that I'm fully willing to let her do this for hours. Then again, I don't think we have that kind of time."

She glanced at Adriana, who shook her head.

"See? We're on a tight schedule, Elman. So, I'm going to have my friend here stop hitting you in the balls because I know that you're going to tell us exactly what we want to know."

He started to shake his head, but June grabbed his jaw and clamped it tight. A new pain shot through his face and skull.

"And I know you're going to do that because if you don't, I am going to let her cut everything off you."

He searched her eyes, his own dancing back and forth trying to pick one that held a different truth than the one she professed. He found no bluff there.

"That's right, Elman. I'll let her start where she wants, too. She might cut those things off first." She tapped on his inner thigh, hinting at what she meant.

He winced at the gesture.

"Of course, I would start somewhere else. Feet are always a good one when it comes to torture."

June produced her pistol and pressed the muzzle into a bone on his right foot. "Have you ever heard someone screaming in agony after being shot in the foot, Elman?" She didn't wait for an answer. "It sounds horrific. I know everyone loves to go for the knees and, don't get me wrong, they're great, too, but there's just something about the feet. Sure makes walking around for the next forty or fifty years a real pain."

"Literally," Adriana added.

June smirked. "Yeah. Literally. Although if you don't tell us after the first foot, we'd go to the second. Then the knees. Eventually, we'd just cut your legs off when we'd used up the pain points on them. That's when we'll go to your fingers and hands. Have you ever seen one of those people that doesn't have hands and arms, Elman?" Her head shook again. "Gotta be a tough way to live. Not to worry, though, we'll be sure to take your eyes and ears, too."

Adriana didn't flinch. She knew June meant every word of it. Anger boiled inside her for the deaths of two of her agents as well as the destruction of their building and the injury of hundreds of other innocent people. That anger drove a freight train loaded with revenge and no brakes straight toward the man in the chair before them.

"You can't do that." Elman's voice trembled, mirroring his quivering lips. "You have rules."

"We don't play by those," Adriana stated. "We make our own."

She let the weapon swing a little closer to his groin, and he shuddered, anticipating the next wave of pain to surge through him. It never came, and he let out a relieved gasp.

"I'd love to show you some pictures of other terrorists we've interrogated in the past," June said, "but I don't keep those around. Legal issues, you see. We enjoy plausible deniability."

"You're crazy. You're both insane!"

June's smirk widened. "Probably. But not telling us where the Teacher is, see, that's even crazier. You tell us where he is, and you keep all those appendages we mentioned before. Or you don't, and you try to go through life without them. It's entirely up to you. Of course, you could die during the process, but I promise you this, Elman..." She leaned close so that her nose was mere inches from his. "We will perform every painful action possible to keep you alive."

His imagination ran wild with more terrible thoughts. *What would they do?* He didn't want to know. Everything she'd said so far was as bad or worse than anything the Red Ring could do to him. He'd heard the stories of some of the people who crossed them. They were killed, sometimes in gruesome ways, but never anything like what she described.

"You're an animal. Animals do things like this."

"No, Elman. Terrorists are animals. And we're the hunters."

She squeezed the trigger, and he grimaced then screamed. It took him a second to realize the weapon wasn't loaded. Mercifully, the gun had merely clicked. The two women frowned as they saw the prisoner's pants soak with urine.

June stood back. "Okay, that is disgusting. What is wrong with you?"

"You were going to shoot my foot!" He added a few unsavory expletives regarding her lineage.

"Yeah, but...just...wow." She turned to Adriana, who'd managed to keep her stoic expression. "What kind of a man pees himself like that?"

"No man I'd ever want." Her response was cold, to the point.

"Okay, your little accident notwithstanding, I think maybe now I should shoot you in the foot just for being a wuss."

"No, please. Please." He shook his head back and forth, causing the chair to almost tip over. "I'll tell you where to find him. He's going to kill you anyway. Might as well let him and his army do it."

"That's better," June said.

"Sort of."

"Yeah, sort of. I mean, still not very nice, but I understand you're upset." She slid a full magazine into the weapon and positioned the gun's muzzle just above his groin. Then she pulled the slide back, chambering a round.

"These .40-caliber hollow points sure do make a mess. I can't imagine what they'd do to your friends down there."

His head shook violently. "The mountains. Okay? He has a palace in the mountains. I can tell you exactly how to get there. I can even show you myself if you want. Please, just don't shoot me."

June frowned. "You could show us?" She glanced over her shoulder at Adriana. "What do you think?"

Adriana's head moved side to side. "No. I don't want the car to smell like urine."

"Good point," June said with a nod. Then she returned her gaze to the prisoner. "Tell me everything."

Elman did as instructed, giving every detail he could muster about how to find the Teacher in his mountain palace, how long it would take to get there, and even the best route to take.

"See? That wasn't so difficult." June said. "But there are still a few things you're leaving out, a few key items."

The cop thought he'd spilled every bean in the bag, desperate to save his skin—and, more importantly, his extremities. "What are you talking about? I told you everything. Please, let me go."

June's head swiveled back and forth.

"I'd like to know how many men they'll have there," Adriana interrupted. "How heavily armed are they? How many rooms are there in this palace? Any secret tunnels for this Teacher to escape undetected? You know, that's the kind of thing I think she meant when she said you're leaving some key items out."

June grinned at the prisoner without looking at her friend. She and Adriana both crossed their arms the same way a schoolteacher would do to a student she knew was lying about something.

He hung his head and thought hard. Sweat rolled down the side of his head and dripped onto the floor. The energy expended during the painful interrogation had caused him to overheat a little.

"Could I get some water or something? It's hot in here."

"Yes, when we're done with you. Then you can have all the water you can stand."

Elman sighed. "I don't know exactly how many rooms. The place has around three stories, but there's a basement, too. Secret tunnels? I don't know if there are or not. He's crafty and paranoid, so I would assume that's certainly possible. His guards are heavily armed, and you can expect to find anywhere from thirty to fifty. Sorry I didn't count them the time I visited. I wasn't really considering an assault on one of the world's most powerful terrorists." He stopped talking and took a deep breath.

"Thank you so much, Elman," June said. "You've been a tremendous help."

She started for the door. Adriana followed.

The Interpol traitor squirmed, rocking the chair back and forth harder. "You said you'd let me go!" he shouted. "And where's my water? Please, I'm so thirsty!"

He almost sounded like a whiny child.

June stopped by the entrance. An old metal case with a large glass covering hung from the wall next to the door. Within, an antique-looking ax dangled from two metal prongs. She couldn't read the words on the cover, but June assumed it said something like "For Emergency Use Only" or "Break Glass in Case of Emergency." There was no emergency at the moment, but the ax would work for her purposes. She smashed the brittle glass with her elbow and used her sleeve to carefully clear away any jagged shards. Then, with an intense glare full of intent and malice, she grabbed the ax and walked over to a pipe that ran along the wall to the prisoner's left. She considered striking the blow behind him where he couldn't see, but then again June wanted this maggot to see exactly what was coming. She wanted him to know terror, anguish, and eventually pain before he succumbed.

"Well, if you want to get technical, we said we'd let you keep your extremities," June corrected. "But we did promise you water, too. Since we didn't say anything about letting you live, I think this is a fitting way for you to go."

The man squirmed and writhed. The chair shivered under the strain of his muscles. It creaked and groaned, but it didn't give.

He swore at the two women, cursing them in multiple languages. Agony stretched across his face, though any pain he was feeling at the moment was self-inflicted: tape cutting into his ankles and wrists, joints pulling to the point of dislocation.

Adriana walked over to a corner where an aged work lamp sat next to a coiled bit of brown extension cord. She picked up the wiring and walked back toward the chair and its prisoner. A dagger sheathed to her side came out quickly with one flick of the wrist. She flayed the wire cover and exposed the thin strands of copper within. Her fingers made quick work of the tiny tendrils, splaying them out like a peacock's feathers, then she dropped the wiring on the floor and padded over to the wall where a socket was fixed into the blocks.

Elman's face filled with panic. He watched with desperation as the Spaniard completed her task, the whole time still struggling to wrestle himself free from the chair.

"Please!" he shouted. "Please, don't do this! I told you everything you wanted to know!"

As was always the case with a coward, he went from outraged demands to fearful groveling. It was a time-honored tradition for that caste of worthless humans. They were full of courage right up to the moment when the executioner lifted the ax. In this case, that was no metaphor.

"You killed innocent people, good agents," June said. "And you helped a known terrorist who's set on killing many more. I hope the money was worth it."

She raised the ax to her shoulder. The old blade displayed a brown patina over most of the metal body, but the sharp edge remained shiny and glistened in the dull glow of the lights.

"What are you..."

Then Elman realized his fate.

Adriana inserted the extension cord into the outlet and stepped toward the door. June didn't say anything else. She swung the blade at the pipe, striking the blow deep into the soft metal pipe. She didn't need to cut through the entire thing, just enough to free the liquid within.

She backed away from the pipe, leaving the ax-head buried halfway in it as the water spewed forth in a dramatic arc that nearly reached the squirming captive.

"No!" He swore again. "Please!"

June strode back to the entrance where Adriana was waiting.

Elman realized that he was in a shallow bowl of sorts, that the room's floor sank in a few inches toward the center. The water was already running toward his chair. Soon, it would pool around his feet. After that, it wouldn't take long before the liquid reached the deadly wires.

"I'll do anything! Take my money! Please!"

"Goodbye, Elman," June said. Her voice carried a spear dipped in venom.

The two women left the room and slammed the metal door shut, muting the screams from beyond.

They bounded up the stairs, back onto the main floor. When they reached the top landing, they hurried over to the computer station and collected a few more things from the crates surrounding the table.

The attack force had stashed a few extra weapons, explosives, and other gear there in case reinforcements were required. Lucky for June and Adriana, Interpol had everything on their grocery list.

They loaded up two gear bags and started for the door. The lights flickered overhead, went black, and then illuminated again. The two women shared a knowing glance.

They hadn't heard the screams of the man down in the basement, but the electrical short signaled what each of them knew.

Elman had just met his end.

23

UZBEKISTAN COUNTRYSIDE

June and Adriana crouched behind a thicket of shrubs perched atop a rise in the foothills of the Chatkal Mountains. They spied the palatial mansion across the ravine. Its white walls glistened in the moonlight.

The two only took a cursory glance at the heavens to appreciate the incredible layout of stars blanketing the night sky above. Without the interference of light pollution, the place gave way to one of the most spectacular views of the stars either had ever seen.

They weren't, unfortunately, on an astronomy mission.

June and Adriana were there to take care of an evil organization who'd managed to spread its tentacles across the globe. Adriana wondered if they were already too late. Despite being able to neutralize much of the threat throughout the civilized world, she couldn't help but think of the rest of the planet, the countries that didn't possess advanced medical techniques or the ingredients necessary to produce the treatment she'd passed on to Johan and his mother in Sweden.

For example, it was likely that a significant portion of Africa would suffer tremendously. Without sufficient resources, entire cities, even nation-states, would crumble. Millions would die within days if they were targeted.

India was another one of the greatest concerns. While in some of the cities many would be treated and relieved of the affliction, the vast majority of the nation was poor and incapable of getting to somewhere they could receive medical attention in time.

China, while highly advanced in many ways, had a massive population that would present near-insurmountable problems for medical personnel.

Between those two nations and the African continent, the death toll could potentially be devastating.

Then there were other pockets where getting care would be problematic. Mexico as well as Central and South America all had locations where medical staffs were either short in number or were working with technologies that badly needed updating.

In the end, reaching a number in the low billions for directly related deaths would be easy.

Adriana shook the thought away. She knew better than to think about things like that. Those factors were out of her hands, if only for a moment. Leaders on every continent had done what they could to warn their populations of the coming threat and how to keep themselves safe from it.

She felt that it wouldn't be enough.

There was still a chance, though—at least she hoped—that if they eliminated the source of the threat, more countries and countless lives could be spared. Within the white walls across the ravine, she knew that source was likely orchestrating his next move.

"I only count five guards on this side of the building," June said, cutting into her partner's thoughts. "Although the slope is steep over here."

"They probably figure no one is stupid enough to try getting up that route."

"Exactly."

"Which is the way we're going to take, isn't it?" The suspicion in Adriana's voice cracked a smile on June's face.

She nodded. "Yup."

From their position, that was going to be the most difficult path. It was also the most direct. Getting around the ravine on the road would take longer. Either way, they would need to travel on foot.

The gravel road wound down the mountain, into the valley below, and then curved back and forth until it reached the huge gates at the front of the mansion. No doubt, the Teacher had positioned the bulk of his security forces there, near the main entry.

The two women were good, but part of being good was knowing which fights to pick. Running headfirst into a swarm of heavily armed terrorists wasn't a solid choice.

Adriana raised her night-vision goggles again and lowered them to the base of the ravine, then slowly traced a dark thread that weaved its way up the hill.

"You see that?" She kept her voice to a dull whisper.

"I see a lot of stuff."

"There's a narrow trail leading up to the northwest corner of the building. Might be a goat path. That's our way up."

June searched the landscape for a moment. "Got it. Yep, that's our way up."

"Now what about our way in?"

The walls surrounding the building were formidable. From their position, the two figured them to be at least twelve feet tall. They had rope in their gear bags, but throwing that over the top would draw attention from anyone on the inside, and based on the intel Elman had so ungenerously given them, it was highly probable more guards were stationed throughout the interior of the heavily defended compound.

"Let's take out those five guards first," June said, making a command decision. "Then we'll address that problem."

Adriana gave a nod.

Action solved problems more often than not. June knew that. They could sit there all night trying to figure out the best solutions, but by then it might be too late. Every second that passed pushed the Teacher's sickening goals closer to fruition.

The two women stuffed their binoculars back into their bags and slung them over their shoulders. Adriana breathed in the dry desert air through her nose, keeping her breaths at an even, calm pace as they made their way between huge boulders, shrubs, and piles of sandy dirt.

The terrain was difficult to navigate. The steep slope made footing tenuous as the soil underfoot slipped and gave way under their weight. Out of necessity, the two women kept their profiles low, crouching as they moved. That served two purposes: keeping their balance, and keeping out of sight.

The air had turned cool after the sun went down, plunging the mountains into a frigid night. Adriana moved through the valley with the stealth of a tiger hunting its prey. It was the way she'd been taught by her father, and by her master, a man who still practiced the ancient way of the Shinobi. She'd never shared that secret with anyone, not even the one man she trusted above all others in her life other than her father.

Sean knew of her skills. He'd seen them in action, witnessed her incredible ability to move among the masses without detection. Her stealth was unmatched, even by him. All the government training in the world hadn't taught him the things she knew, the things she practiced and held secret in the deepest recesses of her soul. She'd shared hints with him, glimpses of her past, but never the ultimate truth. Adriana was an indirect descendant of the ninja, forged in the fires of ancient mountains to the east. Their order was few in number back then, when she was young and still naïve to the world and its evils, and the perils it could fling at human beings.

She learned their history, how they'd morphed into something more than their original purpose. During the days when the Shinobi were at their zenith, they were nothing more than tools of war, weapons against unseen enemies, assassins of the highest power. Those weren't the men and women she learned from. Not anymore. Still deadly, yes, but they had mutated into something that could not only take life but give it, renew it, and ease the suffering of many.

For now, healing was not her primary focus. It was the original purpose that called, the voice of their ancestors that called for the blood of an unseen enemy that justice might prevail.

She crouched low as she pushed up the next hill, her eyes never wavering from the mansion and the five guards that stood on full alert patrolling the ridge above. She didn't need to look to the ground to see the jagged rocks, the scraggly bushes surrounding her. Her feet knew they were there. Her peripheral vision detected everything, even the subtle sounds of June's feet behind her as she followed close behind, rustling loose dirt and sand from the earth.

A single cloud drifted through the sky, momentarily blotting out the light of the moon, casting a dark shadow over the hillside. She picked up her pace, grateful for the temporary camouflage, never once believing it was luck. Her master had taught her there was no such thing as luck, or coincidence. You made your own luck. And fortune, as the old saying went, favored the bold.

Their legs burned as they reached the halfway point up the mountain. The white mansion loomed just ahead, growing larger, more threatening with every step. The cloud overhead floated away from the moon, once more allowing its pale glow to bathe the mountainside in eerie white.

They could see the faces of the men keeping watch now, every detail becoming clearer with each step. The guards were equipped with Kalashnikovs, the typical choice of modern terrorists. The weapons, Adriana and June both knew, were powerful and deadly though difficult to control after the first shot. When used as fully automatic, the barrels tended to rise, the recoil pushing hard against the shooter's shoulder as each successive blast drove the gun's muzzle higher and higher.

Both women had fired the weapons in the past. They likened the guns to riding a bull in a rodeo: difficult to control but incredibly powerful when used properly. Neither had any doubts these guards would have spent countless hours with the weapons and were likely expert marksmen. Such was the enemy they were dealing with. The Red Ring was unlike most terrorist organizations. There was no reason for Adriana and June to assume anything but the worst; that these men were trained killers. Like uncaged lions, these terrorists would need to be treated with the greatest caution.

Adriana pulled the strap around her shoulder a little tighter. The HK-5 she'd procured from Elman's weapons cache hugged her left breast. The elongated barrel of the suppressor dangled slightly but didn't get in her way and, more importantly at the moment, didn't make a sound. She would unleash that beast when the time came.

For now, the Sig Sauer SP2022 in her hand would be more than sufficient. The suppressor made the weapon a little heavy on the front end, but using two hands would help ease that minor problem. She had two additional magazines for it on her left hip, and two for the Heckler & Koch on the back of her belt.

June was similarly equipped. No need for bringing more rounds. They could arm themselves with the weapons of the dead if necessary.

Adriana had spotted their first point of attack near the top of the ridge. A heavy boulder, more than large enough for the two of them to hide behind for cover, would conceal them at the top of the mountain. A zigzagging line of shrubs provided a path to the huge rock that would keep them invisible to the targets, at least for the most part. Between the bushes, they'd have to move quickly, keeping an eye on the men above as they turned their heads from side to side, sweeping the landscape for threats.

As the women reached the first in the crooked line of shrubs, they took quick inventory of the mansion. There were, oddly enough, no cameras positioned in the overhangs of the rooftop. Perhaps that was due to the height of the building. Or maybe the Teacher was simply too cheap to make the investment. Who would think this ivory palace in the middle of the mountains would house the evil within? Overconfidence, it seemed, was a shared genetic trait among villains. A second check in the usual places—corners and atop walls—confirmed the same.

Adriana crouched behind a large shrub and waited, her eyes locked on the guard to the far left. Attacking the man in the center of their line would be catastrophic. It would draw the attention of the four others spaced along the wall and result in gunfire pouring down on them in a handy kill box of their own making. The boulder ahead provided a perfect attack position for the two guards on the left-hand side, while to the right there was nothing but more bushes. It would have to do.

"Take the two on the left. I'll go to the right. Meet me in the center." Her voice came as a snakelike hiss in the night.

June frowned. "There's no cover over there."

"I won't need it. Meet me in the middle."

Before June could protest, Adriana slithered to the next bush, her head still pointing up to the wall and the men guarding it.

June swore under her breath. "No point in arguing," she muttered. Then she took off toward the next shrub, staying as low as she could without having to belly crawl over the rough terrain.

The guards were close now. Both women moved in tandem across the mountain slope. The eyes of the guards remained focused outward, toward the other ridge instead of down the slope. Perhaps they figured something so close would catch their attention. The whites of their eyes glistened in the moonlight, chins remaining raised. The guards were unaware of the deadly danger that loomed just below.

June reached the boulder just thirty feet below the guard to the far left. When she was in position, she glanced back at her friend, who had already arrived at her preferred spot and was on her belly, getting ready to open fire.

Adriana looked back over her shoulder at June and gave a nod. No sense in wasting any more precious time. Now was the moment.

Adriana raised her weapon and looked through the sights at her first target. Death was coming for these evil men on this night, and they would never see it approaching.

June was the first to fire, though only by a fraction of a second. Her weapon discharged with a clack, the suppressor dulling the normally explosive sound of the gun. Suppressors like the ones she and her partner had wouldn't keep the other guards from hearing what was going on. They would know they were being shot at, but the long, cylindrical barrels would dim the noise enough to keep people inside the thick walls from hearing the commotion beyond, and would also protect from potential hearing loss. In stealth situations like this, working quietly was key, which also meant not obstructing one's ears. Hearing the enemy's movements was just as important as keeping them from hearing yours.

The first guards, one on each end, dropped in an instant. Adriana's round pierced the man's throat and dropped him to his knees before he slumped forward, landing on his chest on the edge of the slope.

June's target took the bullet in the skull and collapsed in a heap to his side.

The remaining three guards immediately gripped their weapons tighter and raised them to their shoulders, looking down the sights for the unexpected threat. They swept the range ahead, looking both into the valley below and to the mountain across the ravine, but saw nothing.

Two more shots clapped in the still of the night. Both men on either side of the center guard shuddered from the impact of the rounds as they pierced their bodies—June's through the heart, Adriana's through the forehead. The men fell forward. One toppled clumsily over the edge, his body tumbling down the slope until it came to a stop against a small boulder the size of a wood-burning stove.

The lone remaining guard knew he was in trouble. He couldn't see where the attack was coming from. To him, the assailant was invisible. His weapon, he knew, was useless against such a foe, and he touched a finger to the radio in his ear to call for backup and raise the alarm.

The message never went through.

Adriana and June sprang from their cover, and each squeezed their triggers at the same time, delivering a bullet into the man's chest and right eye socket respectively. He was dead before his body wavered and dropped to the ground.

The women crested the hill and pressed their backs against the wall near their final kill. June watched both ends of the building, her head twisting back and forth as if watching the most intense tennis match of all time. Meanwhile, Adriana bent down and stole the radio from the dead man's ear.

The wall had provided the perfect acoustic deflection for their attack, sending the muffled sounds of their gunshots echoing into the valley below and into the night.

Still, they weren't naïve enough to believe no one had heard their attack. Adriana put the earpiece into her right ear and listened. A man was requesting a reply from the guard, his Arabic calm at first, though with each passing second without an answer his voice grew more concerned.

"We need to move," Adriana said. "They'll send someone out here to check on these five."

June nodded. "Time to go kill the devil."

24

UZBEKISTAN COUNTRYSIDE

The Teacher woke to the sound of a klaxon blaring throughout the compound. His head raised wearily from the soft feather pillow atop the bed and he glanced around the room, still groggy from his deep slumber.

One moment, he was dreaming of eating dates, figs, and nuts while strolling along a sandy beach in what he imagined to be paradise. The next, the world around him plunged into chaos.

The bedroom door burst open.

Aziz stumbled in, a pistol in his hand and a look of desperate concern on his face. "Master!" It was the only word he could manage through the panic in his chest.

The Teacher didn't need to be told anything else. He already knew what his lieutenant was going to tell him. The old man fought through the mind fog, through the doubts, and through all the questions to reach the conclusion he could easily see in Aziz's eyes.

They'd been found. The how didn't matter.

Gunshots at the front gate echoing over the sound of the klaxon confirmed his conclusion. Then the shooting stopped. The Teacher slipped out of his bed and into the leather sandals he usually wore.

He glided over to the window that looked out onto the courtyard and over the front gate toward the distant city of Samarkand. He couldn't see the sprawling town, just the residual light radiating in the sky over the mountains in the distance.

More of his men rushed across the courtyard toward the still-locked gate. He wasn't surprised at the precision with which they moved, their weapons trained on the potential threat just outside of the barricade. They immediately took up a defensive position, ready to funnel the intruders into their snare and cut them down in the crossfire.

The sound of the alarms abruptly ceased. An eerie silence crept over the mansion. The Teacher watched his men holding their positions, waiting for the next move, their eyes fixed on the heavy metal gate. The barrier was made of two solid steel doors with a steel bolt wedged through the center. It was a primitive form of protection against intrusion, he knew, but sometimes the old ways were best. Security systems could be hacked. Automatic gates could have faults. The only way in and out of the compound, as far as most of his men knew, was through the giant steel doors that had to be opened manually. The metal bore no intricate designs, no insignia of his familial lineage. It was functional, nothing more, held in place by huge steel hinges along its edge.

The Teacher waited, his hands resting on the windowsill as he kept his gaze locked on the situation below.

Aziz shifted toward him, stopping a foot behind so he could look over his master's shoulder.

"Do you think they're dead?" Aziz asked. He spoke the words out of hope rather than realism.

The Teacher likewise clung to the same faint hope. His men were good. They'd been trained to take down any attacker who would dare cast their shadow on this mountain. How the these thorns in his side had burrowed so far, he didn't know. The silence, however, didn't carry the same hope, the same reality that he desired. He could feel it. There was a dark, foreboding cloud looming over the mansion, wrapped in the silence of what he feared was the truth.

The deathly still of the night erupted before his eyes.

The wall to the left of his men burst into fiery debris, spraying a deadly hail of concrete, metal, and brick into the courtyard. Eight men were positioned right next to the explosion. They were consumed in a blazing-hot yellow-orange fireball—alive one moment, instantly dead the next.

The blast's concussion rocked the entire compound, shaking the floor under the Teacher's feet, nearly causing him to lose his balance and fall backward into the room. The searing heat climbed into the sky, singeing the old man's skin, causing him to turn his head away for a moment.

The men positioned on the right side of the defensive funnel were ripped apart by the flying stone and metal shrapnel, pelted by thousands of tiny projectiles that struck them in the eyes, the chest, neck, legs, arms. The concussion, too, sucked the air out of their lungs before smashing three of them against the wall behind, tossing them through the air like they were nothing more than a child's rag doll.

The fireball rose into the sky, churning in a soup of boiling black smoke, climbing higher and higher until the pillar blotted out the moon, all within seconds.

The Teacher crouched down, despite the fact it was several seconds too late for that, shielding his face and body from the blast. Aziz instinctively stepped to him, wrapping his arm around the man's shoulders and covering his head and face with his chest as he would a little child who'd just had a nightmare.

When the building ceased its trembling and the sound of the explosion had dissipated into the night, the two men rose again, Aziz letting his leader stand on his own. The two looked out the window and onto the courtyard with horror in their eyes. All sixteen of the men were dead. Eight corpses were visible, unmoving in the carnage of stone, twisted metal, and concrete. The other eight were buried, invisible to the night. They'd been so close to the blast that the Teacher doubted their bodies would ever be found.

That didn't matter now.

He fixed his eyes on the new opening in the wall. The crater stood ten feet high and at least that wide. Amid the smoldering debris, he saw two figures step through with submachine guns pressed against their shoulders, sweeping the area from left to right. Their lithe bodies belied who they were even though the women's faces were covered with black scarves like the ninjas of old.

Four more men poured into the courtyard to the Teacher's left. They charged recklessly ahead, anxious to avenge their fallen brethren and defend the Teacher, who'd given their useless lives a purpose.

The women spun and fired, spraying a blizzard of bullets in their direction, cutting them down with ease. The momentum of the men kept them moving forward even as they fell, dead before they hit the ground.

One of the women looked up at the building, scanning the windows until her eyes met the Teacher's. He could see the whites in the orbs narrow as she realized her target was within reach. Her lightly tanned skin told him exactly who she was. The Spaniard, the woman from the car that should have died in the Liverpool explosion.

The other, too, was a ghost, an impossible apparition that should have only existed in myth. The woman named June Holiday, the leader of the covert agency that had plagued him so greatly over the last year. She should have likewise perished in the second explosion, the one that took out her operation's entire facility.

Yet here they were, two ghosts walking among the living.

It only took a second for June's eyes to also meet his.

The Teacher raised his head in pride, placing both hands on the windowsill.

"Sir!" Aziz said with urgency in his voice. "We must get you to safety. Please."

The Teacher raised his hand to calm the man. "Allah will protect us."

He watched as the women raised their weapons and squeezed the triggers. Bullets pounded the wall around the window. The rapid knocking sounded like a woodpecker pounding away on a tree, hoping to find a meal of grubs within.

Aziz ducked down, afraid he'd be struck in the gunfire, but the Teacher stood unwavering, staring down death in the face as the metal rounds smashed the façade all around him until the women's magazines were spent.

The two shooters stared up at him amid a new haze of gray gun smoke, the last of it trailing out from their muzzles, lingering for a moment around them like an evening mist. Then a light breeze washed over the courtyard and carried it away, mingling it with the smoke still rising into the sky from the explosion.

The Teacher glared at the two attackers with a look of smug confidence. He made no attempt to hide his arrogance. Then, as if they simply weren't there, his eyes wandered to the left, over the western wall to a mountaintop pond that stretched out a hundred yards until it reached the edge of the mountain rimmed by ancient rock. The reservoir had been a source of water for the mansion and allowed the compound to be almost completely self-sufficient. They'd used it to irrigate hydroponic greenhouses within the confines of the structure, growing their own food and providing them with the essentials of life. He gazed at it for a moment in thoughtful reflection and then turned away from the window, leaving the two women staring up in dismay.

He'd known they were barely in range for the weapons in their hands. It would have been sheer luck to hit him with one shot. Combined with the divine protection of his maker, the Teacher knew he would survive the onslaught; and he did.

"Master?" Aziz said, his eyes full of questions. "What will we do now?"

The Teacher offered a kind expression. "The orders have already been given, my Son. Our armies are mobilizing as we speak. Nothing can stop that now."

"But you? You must live."

"I will. And so will you. Come. We have one more surprise in store for these harlots."

Aziz frowned for a moment. Then the lines across his forehead eased as he remembered the fail-safe, the last-ditch plan that they'd prepared in case of such an emergency.

He nodded. "Yes, sir."

25

UZBEKISTAN COUNTRYSIDE

Adriana and June sprinted through the vast halls of the mountain compound. They kicked open doors to cells and swept each room to make certain no other members of the Red Ring were lurking in the shadows to ambush them.

As they reached a corner at the end of the first floor, Adriana poked her weapon around the edge, then her head. A loud pop reverberated, followed by several more. She ducked back just in time, aided by June pulling on her shoulder to get her clear of the line of fire.

The two pressed their backs against the wall and readied their weapons. They'd already loaded full magazines after failing to take out the Teacher, but the man had disappeared from view and was on the run. If he got away, everything they'd worked for would crumble. All their efforts, their research, tracking, the lives sacrificed would be in vain, and the hunt would start all over again.

"I count six." Adriana said.

June nodded and reached into her satchel. She pulled out a small round disk about the size of a quarter and pressed her thumb into it, clicking it three times. Then she flung it around the corner with a backhanded toss and retreated a second before a bright white light flashed through the corridor.

Men screamed.

Then the two women stepped out from their cover and leveled their weapons. The terrorists were covering their eyes. Some had dropped their guns. One was looking around in temporary darkness, his retinas burning from the flash bang's searing light.

The hallway filled with the muted clapping of submachine guns as the women opened fire, tearing through the ranks of the enemy in short bursts of hot metal.

They didn't stop moving even as the men fell in a pile at the bottleneck of the corridor. Jumping over them, Adriana and June kept pushing ahead, charging down the passage toward the other end of the building. They knew the Teacher wouldn't remain upstairs. He was a coward; that much was clear. He would try to run, just as he had in Liverpool.

That didn't mean they couldn't flush him in the direction they wanted him to go.

June reached into her satchel and pulled out two more charges. The powerful Semtex in the devices was more than enough to bring down part of the compound's wing. It was what they'd used in taking out the wall to gain entry. By planting a few well-placed charges, they could weaken or even collapse part of the building, thus forcing the Teacher to take the route they desired.

Adriana took out two of her own charges and placed them on the opposite wall, then planted a third and fourth on a load-bearing beam.

With their explosives set, the two took off again back in the direction they'd come from to get clear of the blast. They'd positioned the charges at the end of the building, knowing (or hoping) that they would bring down only a third of the structure. Then again, without the schematics and details of the construction, it could be more or less. More wouldn't be a problem unless it was a lot more. They still had two more explosives each with which they could severely weaken the rest of the building, though it might require more firepower to take down the entire thing. It was anyone's guess.

They reached the middle of the compound, running by an area that housed a huge cafeteria with dozens of wooden tables and benches where the Red Ring's recruits could eat their meals together.

Adriana paused for a fleeting second to take in the dramatic domed ceiling with black metal chandeliers hanging along the center beam at twenty-foot intervals. She scanned the room to make sure there were no stragglers from the Teacher's personal guard and then kept moving.

They reached a split in the hallway where paths shot off to the right and left as well as straight ahead to the end of the compound where a closed door was set in the wall. To their left, a foyer opened up with a wide stairwell leading up to the higher levels. To the right, a door opened to what was likely the outer wall and a patrol path that encircled the compound.

There were no ornate paintings or decorations on the interior of the corridor, only black sconces with unlit candles, reminiscent of an ancient castle.

"He'll come down these stairs," June said. "Hold here and cover me. When he shows his ugly mug, I'll take the shot."

Adriana confirmed the order with a nod and crouched next to her friend as June pulled out her remote detonator, a small black box with a switch and a button concealed by a plastic safety cap. She flipped the switch and opened the cap, ready to press it when Adriana raised her hand.

"Wait."

The Spaniard had been sweeping the corridor, looking down each path to make sure they weren't caught off guard, when she caught a glimpse of something in the doorway at the end of the compound. There was a small square window with four iron bars across it. On the other side, she saw a face. It was one she recognized. Old eyes stared out at her, narrowed in anger but also displaying another sentiment. Was it mischief?

Then she realized what it was. The expression was one she'd seen before, one she recalled from her training when her master knew he was about to get the better of her, even as she moved in for a strike.

The Teacher, it seemed, had a backup plan in place.

"What?" June looked over at her, thumb on the button.

"He's getting away. End of the hall through that doorway."

June glanced in that direction but didn't see anything. The Teacher had disappeared.

"Come on," Adriana urged, charging ahead once more as she fought against the burning in her legs from all the running and the climb up the mountain.

"What about the charges?"

Adriana skidded to a stop and looked back over her shoulder. She heard men shouting from the other end of the building. They must have been stationed upstairs and were coming in to reinforce the rest of the terrorists. "Blow them."

June stepped out from the corner, started jogging toward her friend, and then depressed the button.

As the sudden boom echoed through the building, the two instantly took off at a sprint again, darting to the end of the hall toward the door. The blast was deafening, even though it was on the far side of the building. The entire compound shook. The floor under their feet buckled, but they didn't stop until they reached their destination. Adriana twisted the knob and flung the door open as a cloud of gray dust rolled down the corridor behind them, chasing them like some ghastly monster of ancient lore.

June shoved through the opening first, sweeping her gun left and right. "Clear!" she shouted.

Adriana didn't have to be told what to do next as the dust cloud continued plowing toward them. She ducked inside behind her friend and slammed the door shut mere seconds before the monster reached them, sealing off any potential dust or debris that could seep in.

The compound rumbled around them, shaking loose fragments from the spiral staircase in which they now stood. The stone steps led up and down, but the two women knew the old man wasn't going up.

There was no helipad up there for him to use as a means of escape. The only way out was down.

The pushed ahead through the dimly lit passage. Bulbs flickered along the walls and then went black as the power to the building was lost in the explosion and subsequent destruction.

June paused, fished out a light from her bag, and then attached it to her pistol, tightening the submachine gun to her torso once more. Adriana did the same. Their lights bloomed to life and cast bright, wide circles on the wall and steps below.

They couldn't hear movement due to the crashing and trembling around them. Both wondered if this part of the building would hold up. Without being able to see what was going on outside the staircase, it was anyone's guess.

June and Adriana bounded down the stairs, taking two at a time, careful not to slip as they pressed faster and faster. The old man wouldn't be quick, but he had a head start.

After descending what seemed like four stories into the mountain, they reached a landing where a heavy wooden door stood open. June paused for a moment and peeked around the corner. A gun popped a warning from somewhere in the darkness beyond, and she ducked back as the bullet ricocheted off the stone wall in a miniature cloud of dust.

The rumbling began to settle. The damage above had been done and was now quieting down to a dull tremor.

Footsteps on the other side of the wall signaled their quarry was on the move again. Emboldened by the sound of retreat, Adriana eased through the opening, leading with her pistol and bright light, and nosed her way around the corner. She saw two figures sprinting back toward the other end of the mountain, below where the building had collapsed.

As June joined her in the underground chamber, they realized the compound had been built atop a cave.

Stalactites and stalagmites ran along the far wall, showing themselves in the white glow of their lights, glistening with moisture from underground veins of water that dripped onto them. The women detected the faint sound of water trickling somewhere in the darkness but didn't see where the ancient river flowed or if that was indeed what they heard.

Their focus shifted instantly to the enemy, who continued running down the length of the cave. Adriana and June were standing on a narrow path that ran the length of the foundation wall to their left. Whoever built this place had an escape plan in mind. Whether it was the Teacher or not, they didn't know, and it didn't matter. The end was in sight, and it was time to make the old man pay for what he'd done.

Adriana darted ahead with June just behind her. They breathed hard in the moist cavern air, careful not to slip on the wet surface at their feet. Where were these two going? Who was the man with the Teacher? It must have been his second-in-command, a personal bodyguard.

The two men were hindered by the old man's inability to move quickly, and the women closed the gap with every step.

There was no light at the end of the tunnel, which meant there was no escape, no hope for the Teacher now. He was running headlong into a trap of his own making.

What had been a fifty-yard head start was now down to twenty, and the old man was clearly running out of energy. He stumbled at one point, and June took a shot, the round pinging off the ceiling as her barrel bounced along wildly in her hand.

The Teacher collected himself and kept moving, though slower and slower with each passing second.

When the gap had closed to fifteen yards, the young guard stopped and urged his leader onward, spinning around to face the oncoming threat. He crouched to one knee, raised a pistol, and squeezed the trigger.

The rounds fired true, narrowly missing the women as they were forced to dive to either side. Adriana jumped to the right and rolled up onto one knee, shining her bright light into the shooter's eyes. The man winced.

On the other side of the path, June rolled onto her belly, steadied her weapon, and squeezed the trigger three times.

The bullets peppered the man's body, an easy target for her at that distance as he crouched in the open, his frame illuminated by the two flashlights on their weapons.

One round struck his knee, the second his sternum, and the third in the upper left part of his chest. He howled, his body contorting back in an awkward twist, and then fell on his back.

Adriana risked a quick glance back to make sure there were no other men following them, and then stood, keeping her weapon trained on the guard's body. She noted the sound of water next to her, rushing along the side of the path. An underground river of sorts. Then she moved ahead to the fallen bodyguard.

June reached her victim at the same time and stared down at the man whose blank eyes stared off into the darkness. His chest rose once, fell, and then went still. Blood seeped from the wounds, but the one that killed him was the one in his chest, a bullet straight into his heart.

"Check him," Adriana said. "I'm going after the Teacher."

June nodded and bent down to search the guard.

Adriana took off again, running harder than she'd ever run in her life. She could see the man's robes flowing in the breeze as he charged forward into the ever-narrowing corridor.

She'd gone another fifty yards when she realized the cavern was closing into a horizontal cone shape.

The Teacher stopped at the end where the wall closed. There was nowhere to run.

"Put your hands up!" she shouted when she was a mere thirty feet away. Her gun trained on the center of his spine, the broad circle of light covering him and a good five feet on either side.

The man kept his hands to the side for a moment and then slowly began to raise them, albeit with great reluctance.

"Turn around," she ordered.

A sickly laugh echoed off the ancient stone in front of his face, reverberating back to her with an eerie overtone, much like a storm cloud cresting a mountain, ready to wreak havoc on the valley below.

"I said turn around," Adriana said in Arabic.

Another laugh. Then: "You think you are so clever, you whore." The man's reply came likewise in the same language. "You are too late. Even as we speak, my army of Allah's warriors prepares their assault on the world. Millions will die. My death is of no consequence. My mission has been fulfilled, as has the will of my god."

"I said turn around." She ignored his retort and the insult.

"Of course."

He twisted slowly, his wrinkled, bearded face revealed in the white glow of her light. A wicked smile creased his lips.

"On your knees."

He raised an eyebrow. "Ah, but that will never happen," he said in heavily accented English. "I will never bow to a harlot like you." She lowered the weapon and put her sights on a bulge in the middle of his leg. She fired.

The round pierced his knee, shattering the cap into bloody fragments, dropping the Teacher to the ground.

He gasped but didn't scream. He would give her no such pleasure. His left hand grabbed at the wound, though, which was enough for her.

Adriana stepped toward him, approaching him as she would a wounded venomous serpent, its fangs dripping with death, still capable of delivering a mortal bite.

Even as he writhed, he looked into the light of her beam with a sickly grin.

"What are you going to do, whore? Arrest me?" He chuckled through crooked teeth, his eyes full of a mad look only seen in the most secret rooms of asylums.

She shook her head. "No. We don't arrest people like you. We make examples to others who would take up your flag and threaten the innocent."

Another laugh.

"You think I fear death? I will be in paradise this day. You? You will not."

Adriana frowned at the statement. There was something about it, something sinister. A clue perhaps?

She got her answer as her eyes wandered to his other hand. A small metal box rested in his palm, thumb on a red button.

His eyes narrowed as he widened his smile. She raised her pistol to his head to fire, but the old man's thumb sank into the device.

A crack came from overhead, back in June's direction. Then a loud boom. She looked back at where her friend was crouching over the dead guard. "Run!"

June stood immediately and looked around. Then she took off in the other direction, back toward the stairwell.

Adriana returned her gaze to the Teacher. His laughter swelled, mingling with the chain of explosions in the ceiling above, even as huge chunks began falling around them.

"Time to burn," he said.

Adriana squinted at him. "You first." She squeezed the trigger. A pink mist sprayed out of the back of his skull onto the cave wall. His body went limp, unlike the shuddering cavern around them.

Massive chunks of rock collapsed from above, cutting off the path to the exit. There was no way out.

Or was there?

Adriana remembered the sound of the water to her right. She retreated a few steps as a giant stalactite fell from the roof and crashed into the path mere feet from her. She pointed her light onto the floor and raised it slowly, letting it play across the stone until she saw what she was looking for.

The cavern's river was only four feet wide, at best, but she traced it to the wall near where the dead leader of the Red Ring lay, the water cutting through a narrow opening in the stone.

Then another sound joined in the cacophony. Enormous amounts of water rained down from above, first at the other end of the cave, then flooding in from every weakened spot where the explosives had done their work.

The Teacher had lured them into a trap. His plan was never to escape. It was to eliminate the last threat to his plan. He was going to flood the cavern.

26

UZBEKISTAN COUNTRYSIDE

Adriana took two quick steps and leaped into the river as the cascade of water showered down from above amid falling rock.

She plunged sideways into the cold river. A stalactite shot through the liquid next to her, scraping her shoulder and sending a sudden surge of icy-hot pain through her nerves. She didn't have time to hurt.

With the gun still in her hand, she wrestled the flashlight free and wedged it into her mouth then dropped the weapon, letting it float to the bottom of the cave river.

Her arms pulled against the water, hands acting like paddles as she swam hard toward the opening. Her legs kicked. The current of the little river wasn't strong, but at least it was helping.

With the first wave of water from above, she felt an abrupt surge blast her toward the opening. Then came a horrific realization, the new water was lifting her toward the cavern wall. She was going to miss her target.

The powerful uplift drove her against the jagged wall, twisting her around a split second before she hit. Her back struck first, sending a dull pain through her spine. Her skull smacked against it, dizzying her. The flashlight dropped out of her mouth and into the current below. The cavern flooded quickly, the tide rising with incredible and deadly speed.

Adriana shook her head to loosen the cobwebs, but that only made things worse. The water pressed against her with the strength of a bulldozer for a few horrible seconds, and then it relented.

The one good thing the surge had done was drive her back up into the air where she could regain her breath, but now the rising tide was filling the cavern. The ceiling above was growing ever closer at an alarming rate. She flapped her arms downward to stay afloat as the pressure against her body receded. Within seconds, though, she'd have no more air to breathe. She looked down into the water and saw her flashlight carried away through the canal in the wall, its beam still bobbing and dancing in the darkness. If she was going to get out of here alive, she had to move now. No chance she'd get out if the light was gone.

Mind made up, Adriana dove down into the flood, following the gyrating beam as it dimmed, signaling its passage into the underground river tunnel. She kicked her feet and pulled with her hands, swimming hard toward the light.

Suddenly, a heavy rock plunged into the water from above and dove toward her. She heard the sound but didn't see the threat until it was too late. A last-ditch twist to the right kept the bulk of the stone from pinning her chest to the floor, but it caught her right foot and pulled it downward, causing her body to flip out of position.

The light grew dimmer in the tunnel below, and she knew time was almost gone.

Adriana flipped herself around and swam harder, pulling her body through the water. Another crash echoed through the new underground lake, and she knew more of the ceiling had collapsed.

She dipped her head lower and kept swimming, knowing what was to come.

This time, another surge pushed her forward, but she'd swum low enough that the uplift lined her up almost perfectly with the tunnel opening.

She shot forward at a reckless pace, guiding her momentum with hands and feet. The tunnel's narrow, jagged opening loomed just ahead, rushing toward her. If she struck it with her head, that would be the end.

Fortunately, Adriana saw the danger and maneuvered her body, contorting it just enough to dodge the hard, sharp edges.

She catapulted through the opening and into the tube, the pressure of the lake behind her surging her forward faster than she could have ever done on her own.

Up ahead, her flashlight was wedged against a piece of rock that jutted up from the riverbed. She stuck her right hand down as she passed over it and scooped it up, not sure if she needed it but taking comfort in what little light it could shed on the gloom around her.

The current carried her forward at an incredible pace now, but she had enough control to kick and drive her body upward to where she hoped there would be enough of a gap to take a quick breath.

Her head burst through the surface into a domed opening where there was still air. Despite the immense pressure from the flooded cavern, the river could only take so much, which meant any air shafts that had been there before would still be present.

Her respite only lasted a few fleeting seconds as the current again pushed her toward another tunnel. She hit the wall with a thud, still clutching the light in one hand, bracing against the impact with her feet.

Then she felt the ripping current pull her down again. With a last gasp, Adriana was tugged under.

Instead of fighting it, she knew what to do. She pushed out from the rock and let the underground river take her, pushing her through the next opening into another shaft.

The sides of the tunnel scraped against her skin. She couldn't see in the debris all around her. The light in her hand was almost useless, merely casting an amorphous glow into the liquid haze that embraced her and carried her ever forward.

Something hard struck her elbow and sent a surge of pain through the bone, loosening her fingers' tenuous grip on the light.

The device flew away from her, drifting down the shaft faster than she could go. It banged against something in the distance, and then it was gone.

Adriana was bathed in darkness. Her lungs screamed for more air, aching and contracting with every second.

She had one terrible thought that hung in her mind like a cloud in the sky to the victim of an executioner. *Sean would never know what happened to her.*

Then, as she readied herself to take her last breath, one that would fill her lungs with a liquid that would squelch her life from this earth, she felt something strange. The water that wrapped around her let go, replaced by...nothing.

Everything around her was still dark, but she felt herself falling, surrounded by water, yes, but in an ever-dissipating mist. She was in midair.

The sensation only lasted a couple of seconds before she felt her feet hit the surface of more water. A quick gasp filled her lungs enough to survive the plunge as she sank into a new body of liquid. Downward she went until her feet hit something solid. The current was gone, replaced by a churning overhead and behind her. She pressed her boots into the ground, driving her body upward. Her hands pulled, grasping at the water like a rock climber surging to the summit.

Then her head burst through the surface and into the night air. Her mouth opened, taking in huge gulps of air, lungs filling gratefully. She breathed hard while at the same time twisting her head around to gain her bearings. Thirty feet above, a waterfall dumped the contents of the cavern out of the mountain into a shallow lake.

Adriana noted a shoreline to her right and swam toward it even as relief spilled into her mind. Her back ached. The pain in her elbow still resonated through her arm and up to her shoulder, but she didn't care. She was alive.

She reached the rocky beach and struggled on hands and knees until she was completely out of the water. Then she slumped down on her side and let her head fall onto one arm. A moment later, she rolled onto her back and looked up into the sky, the blanket of stars twinkling overhead as confirmation that she wouldn't die this day, that she would remain among the land of the living. Then she closed her eyes and said a grateful thank-you to the heavens.

27

SAMARKAND

June sat in the waiting room of the hospital, staring at her phone. She'd been waiting for her friend to be released for the last couple of hours.

Adriana had fractured her elbow and would be in a cast for the next six weeks or so, but she'd be okay—other than some heavy bruises on her back and a mild concussion. Nothing the Spaniard hadn't been through before.

June hadn't wanted to abandon her friend in the cavern, but there hadn't been a choice. The explosions in the ceiling above signaled only one decision, and it was one both women knew had to be made.

Before running back to the secret staircase, June had searched the Teacher's second-in-command, finding a cell phone and a few other items of interest. She stuffed them in her pockets just moments before the ceiling collapsed. When she reached the safety of the surface, she lamented the fact that Adriana had given her life to make certain the Teacher would not live to see another day. Guilt had riddled her. Tears had streamed from her eyes.

But June was a professional. Despite the tsunami of emotions, she knew there was still one more thing to do, and the things she'd taken from the Teacher's bodyguard might be just what she needed to do it.

She'd opened the device's text message application and discovered the most recent message was sent to dozens of numbers at once, all with the same attack orders. Amid the tears and heavy breathing, June risked sending out a new order, one that told the other cells to stand down and cease their attacks. She also ordered them to return to the palace, the mountaintop compound—or what was left of it. One by one, the men in charge replied with confirmation that they would abort their attacks and return to headquarters.

June didn't know how long it would take them all to get back, but she assumed at least a few hours.

She'd sat there on the rocky ground in the compound's courtyard, staring at the rubble around her. Only the part of the building that housed the staircase and a small section of the passageway leading to it remained; the rest had been destroyed by her explosives.

For thirty minutes, June let herself cry, mourning the loss of her friend, until she heard a strange noise from the new opening in the wall. She spun around with her weapon raised, ready to eliminate the new threat, but instantly lowered the weapon when she saw the apparition.

It was Adriana.

She was bleeding, soaking wet, and looked like a cat that just came in from a thunderstorm, but she was alive.

A message popped up on June's phone as she recounted the events in her mind. No one else was in the waiting room, so she didn't worry with hiding her screen from anyone.

Twelve more apprehended.

She grinned. Groups of the Red Ring's soldiers had been returning to the mountaintop base over the last twenty-four hours. They had no idea they were running headlong into a trap until it was too late. The wreckage of their precious leader's mansion only furthered their curiosity. By the time they realized what had happened, they were surrounded by Pavard's Interpol units and taken into custody.

So far, they'd managed to corral more than two hundred terrorists, with more still likely to come.

Double doors in the hallway burst open, and Adriana appeared in a wheelchair pushed by a nurse.

She wheeled by the windows in front of the waiting room and waved the nurse away, insisting that she was fine on her own. The man relented and went back through the doors, disappearing down the next hallway.

Adriana looked through the glass and offered a weak smile. June returned the gesture.

With some considerable effort, Adriana pushed herself out of the wheelchair. June bounced out of her seat, eager to help her friend. She hurried out the door, but it was too late. Adriana was already on her feet.

They'd already exchanged hugs and tears the night before in the Chatkal Mountains. Now they simply exchanged a subtle glimpse of pride.

"So," June said.

"So."

"What's next?"

"I was going to ask you the same thing." Adriana raised her arm wrapped in a pink cast. "I think I'll have to take some time off."

June chuckled. "I see you went with the pink."

Adriana bit her lower lip. "It's what they had."

"I wonder what Tommy or Sean would do if they were put in a pink cast."

The two of them laughed hard for a minute at the thought.

Then June swallowed hard, looked down at the floor, and then up to her friend's eyes. "They've brought in a few hundred terrorists and more are coming every day. The world is going to be safe...for now."

"That's good." Adriana paused. "What about Shadow Cell?"

June drew in a long breath of the sterile air that reeked of cleaners. She exhaled. "For now, I don't know. We'll be down for a while. I'm actually okay with that. I miss Tommy."

Adriana's eyes squinted as she grinned. "I know the feeling."

"I think Pavard and the rest of the world's anti-terrorist agencies can handle things for now. The real question is what we tell Sean and Tommy we've been up to for the last several months. Lie to them?"

Adriana snorted. "I think we both know that's not possible."

"Indeed."

"Although I'm not sure how I'm going to explain this broken arm to Sean."

"Just tell him the truth."

Adriana's grin twisted to a confused scowl.

"That you were in a cave and fell, hit your arm really hard," June clarified. "He knows you're into extreme stuff like that."

The smile on Adriana's face returned.

"True."

There was a moment of awkward silence between them, as if pondering what to say next.

June spoke first. "Thank you, for everything. You have helped make the world a safer place. You didn't have to do that."

Adriana glanced down at her feet and then back up at her friend. "Yes, I did."

Silence returned to the corridor.

"You going to be okay?" Adriana asked after a contemplative moment. "What's your next move?"

"Shadow Cell is being investigated by the British government. They want to know what happened and how."

"An investigation?"

"Don't sound so worried. They won't find anything. A little misdirection goes a long way." June stretched her arms and yawned. "The mind is an easy enough thing to manipulate. People will believe what you want them to."

"You make it sound so sinister."

June shrugged. "It is, I suppose, but we're the good guys. Some things are best left out of the public eye. Would do more harm than good. As for my plan, I don't know yet. I have a feeling Shadow Cell will be shut down. At least for a while. I'll travel. Spend some time with Tommy. Take it easy for a bit."

Adriana nodded absently. "You know how to do that?"

They shared a laugh.

"What about you?" June asked. "What's your next move?"

"Well, while you're winding things down back in Great Britain, I'm going to track down Sean, see what he's up to."

"Any idea where he is?"

Adriana pursed her lips and shook her head. "No. But I have a feeling it won't be too difficult to figure out."

THANK YOU

As always, I want to say thank you for reading this story. I love creating stories that entertain people. It's truly the best job in the world for me. So, thank you again for spending your time with one of my stories. I appreciate it.

For more great stuff, exclusive content, and updates, visit ernestdempsey.net.

Ernest

ACKNOWLEDGMENTS

As always, I would like to thank my terrific editors for their hard work. What they do makes my stories so much better for readers all over the world. Anne Storer and Jason Whited are the best editorial team a writer could hope for and I appreciate everything they do.

I also want to thank Elena at L1 Graphics for her tremendous work on my book covers and for always overdelivering. Elena definitely rocks.

Last but not least, I need to thank all my wonderful fans and especially the advance reader team. Their feedback and reviews are always so helpful and I can't say enough good things about all of them.

A very special thank you to one of my long-time readers, Dr. Alan Fixelle, for his thoughts and contributions through the years, but especially for this book. I appreciate it, Doc.

OTHER BOOKS BY ERNEST DEMPSEY

The Secret of the Stones

The Cleric's Vault

The Last Chamber

The Grecian Manifesto

The Norse Directive

Game of Shadows

The Jerusalem Creed

The Samurai Cipher

The Cairo Vendetta

The Uluru Code

The Excalibur Key

The Denali Deception

The Sahara Legacy

The Fourth Prophecy

Adriana Villa Adventures:

War of Thieves

When Shadows Call

Shadows Rising

ABOUT THE AUTHOR

Ernest Dempsey is from Chattanooga, Tennessee where he still calls home after 42 years. He's written and published more than 30 books and is always creating more. He loves watching football, soccer, hockey, and baseball when he's not writing and also playing the occasional video game. If you're ever in Chattanooga, feel free to reach out and say hi. You never know, Ernest might meet up with you for a cup of coffee.

Ernestdempsey.net

Published in the United States of America by 138 Publishing.

Made in the USA
Las Vegas, NV
22 February 2022